The Crush

The Crush

Alex Shearer

Hodder
Children's
Books

a division of Hachette Children's Books

First published in paperback in Great Britain
by Hodder Childrens Books in 1998
This edition published in Great Britain
in 2003 by Hodder Children's Books

5

A Catalogue record for this book
is available from the British Library

ISBN-10: 0 340 88207 7
ISBN-13: 9780340882078

Typeset by Hewer Text Ltd, Edinburgh
Printed and bound in Great Britain by
Clays Ltd, St Ives plc

The paper and board used in this paperback by Hodder Children's
Books are natural recyclable products made from wood grown in
sustainable forests. The manufacturing processes conform to the
environmental regulations of the country of origin.

Hodder Children's Books
A Division of Hachette Children's Books
338 Euston Road
London NW1 3BH

1

THE BEGINNING

She knew it was love. It had to be. It couldn't be anything else.

"Come on, Ally," her mother tried to persuade her. "Be reasonable. How can you honestly be in love with someone you've never even met? You can't be really. You're just imagining it, don't you think?"

Only what was the difference between being in love and thinking you were in love? Explain that one.

Anyway, that was a big mistake to start with: confiding in your mother. You might as well tell your sister.

"Him? He'd never fancy *you!*" Cheryl said. "He's got half the country to choose from. Supermodels and all sorts, he goes out with. So why should he bother with you? No, I tell you, a lot of girls would have to die of strange diseases before you got to the front of the queue, Ally Morgan. Huh!"

So that was another mistake as well.

"Thanks for nothing, Cheryl," she told her, getting all saddled up on the old high horse. "And I'll thank you to remember that my name's not Ally, it's Alice." Though everyone called her Ally and had done since she was born, and she had never objected before.

You could always tell a friend about it, of course, but there were risks even there.

Everything you say may be taken down and used in evidence against you at a later date as they said in the police series. And some friends were like that too. Every secret you told them would be taken down and remembered and possibly used against you at some time in the future, when you least wanted your secrets to come out.

You only had to fall out with your best friend for five minutes and there it was: ALICE MORGAN LOVES MATTHEW FRY, all over the blackboard. And she hadn't loved him at all. Not even fancied him, not that much. Didn't even know why she'd said it, to be honest. Just the sort of thing you say when someone asks you who you like and you feel that you ought to have someone. But this – this was different. This was the real thing.

This was love.

"I felt the same way myself once, over David Cassidy," her mum admitted, the first time Ally tried to tell her about it. (David *who*? Ally thought) "I was one of those screaming girls, I remember," her mum said. "All waiting at the back door of the theatre to chase after his car when he came out. And what would we have done if we'd ever caught him . . ."

"Ripped them to shreds, probably," Ally's dad said. And he sounded a bit disappointed that a crowd of screaming girls hadn't ripped him to shreds once, when he had been younger.

"But when you get up close, you know," Mum continued, "most pop stars really don't look much different from anyone else."

"Oh, but Stevie Manns does," Alice sighed. "He's so . . . I don't know . . . handsome."

"He looks like an undercooked teacake to me," her dad muttered. "And what's that on his chin?" he asked. "Is it bum fluff? Or is he trying to grow a beard? Because if he is, he's not making a very good job of it. He'll need another ten years at that rate before he needs to buy a razor."

"You," Alice said, "just don't understand. You've forgotten how to understand. And you know why?"

"No," her mum said. "Tell us."

"Because," said Alice, with all the disdain she could muster, "you've got too old!"

And she swept from the room.

But instead of her words having the effect she had intended, her mum and dad collapsed with good humoured laughter.

But they *didn't* understand. They couldn't. They *were* too old. Not that old, but you didn't have to be. Even the wrong side of twenty was far enough away to be out of touch.

No, it wasn't that kind of love Alice was talking about.

It was great love. Romeo and Juliette love. The sort of love that filled you when Stevie Manns took his solo spot to sing *All Together In My Heart* and when you knew he was singing it just for you alone.

It was uncanny as well, the way his eyes followed you when he was on the television. Alice had heard about pictures in galleries doing that, but never of someone on the television doing it before. It was as if he could see her just the same way she could see him. As if he could see right into the living room. As if he was almost reaching out for her hand – no, holding it – as he sang:

"All together in my heart
You'll see we two will never part . . ."

And the other three members of the group – Nitz (the bad one with the tattoo) and Charlie (the tall, gangly one) and Bobby R (the one with the long hair who was a bit on the chubby side, not fat though, but just cuddly) – they all went:

"Chuggy-chug-chuggy
Chag a woo-ahh!"

And it was enough to melt your heart.

As long as you were left alone in the room to enjoy it of course. But if Mum and Dad were watching too, or if Gran had called round, or if any grown-up was present at all, it spoilt the whole thing.

All you got were the non-stop comments and the stupid remarks.

4

"What does he think he looks like?"

"Look at that earring in his nose. He looks like he escaped from a pig farm."

(*Oh, ho, ho! Pardon me while I laugh till I'm sick.*)

"And look at those trousers – well, if you can call them trousers! Indecent is what I call them."

"And it's not as if it's even proper *music*."

(*Thank you*, Gran. *And how would you know? You don't have your hearing aid on half the time anyway and we all have to shout.*)

"They should learn to play those instruments before they make the next record. If there's going to be a next record. And let's hope there isn't."

"It's all miming anyway. It's not them doing it at all."

And so it went on, all that predictable, grown-up stuff. And they had. They'd just all forgotten. Forgotten what it was like to be young.

And in love.

Just a crush indeed. How dare anyone call it that, what Alice and Stevie felt for each other. You might as well call a mountain a molehill, or the sun a light bulb, as to give such a small name as a crush to a thing as big as their romance.

But sometimes it did crush you, that feeling. It was like an elephant sitting on your chest. It made it difficult to breathe – especially when Ally lay in bed, looking up

5

at Stevie's face on all the posters that covered the ceiling and the walls, and especially when he sang:

"All together in my heart,
You'll see we two will never part.
Let me take you in my arms,
We can't come to any harm . . ."

for the umpteenth time that day.

She knew what being crushed meant then.

Ah yes. There it was again. The inevitable knock on the living room ceiling.

"Turn that flipping stereo down, can't you? I can't hear myself pick my lottery numbers."

(*Can't hear yourself pick your nose more like.*)

"Ally! Is that the only record you've got! Can't you play another one?"

"All right, all right, I'll listen to it on the headphones."

"Well not too loud, or you'll damage your ears."

Her ears! Her ears! Was she seriously supposed to worry about damaging her ears when unrequited love was damaging her heart? What were sore ears when love was at stake. She'd gladly have put up with a million throbbing eardrums, with a million splitting headaches, just for one moment with Stevie, just to be near to him as he sang:

"Let me take you in my arms
We can't come to any harm."

And he could. That would be all right. She'd let him –

maybe – take her into his arms so that they could be sure not to come to any harm together, ever. And she never would come to any harm again. And not even Marlene Forrester would be able to get to her. In fact when Marlene Forrester got to hear about Stevie Manns taking Alice Morgan in his arms and making sure she didn't come to any harm, then Marlene Forrester would be pigsick, good and proper. And serve her right. Because nobody in their right mind would want to take Marlene Forrester into their arms. Put their hands round her neck and squeeze, maybe. But take her into their arms? No. The only thing you'd want to do with Marlene Forrester would be to stick her in a black dustbin liner and drop her into the nearest wheelie bin on the morning of collection day.

Now what was it he sang next? The rest of the verse?
"Let me take you in my arms,
We can't come to any harm.
Let me kiss your fingertips,
Let me hold them to my lips."
Ally went sort of hot and cold at that. Knowing, and yet not knowing. Wanting, and yet not wanting. A little excited and a little nervous too. A little afraid. Because the arms bit, well, that was okay. You knew about arms and being safe from harm. It was like her dad had done when she had been small and had had nightmares. She'd cry for him and he would come and tell her there was

nothing to worry about and it was all going to be all right
. . . all the old familiar words he always said.

He'd put on the lights, and open the cupboard and the
wardrobe door.

"See, Ally, see. There are no monsters. It's all right. It's
just a dream."

"Pick me up, Dad, just for a minute."

Yes. You could understand. Looking back, you could.
And yet, when Ally saw her father now, she wondered a
little. He had seemed so big and strong back then, as if
he could have strangled any monsters and frightened
any burglars away. But now she realised that in fact her
dad wasn't all that big, or all that strong. . . . He was
more sort of well . . . ordinary. Anyway, someone else
had come along now.

"Let me kiss your fingertips,
Let me hold them to my lips."

Yes. Kissing fingertips. Holding them to his lips. That
was all a bit new and scary. And yet, if Stevie Manns
actually asked if he could please kiss her fingertips and
hold them to his lips as well, what was she going to do
about that? Was she going to let Stevie kiss her fingertips
or wasn't she?

Well now. That was a big and burning question.
Maybe she wouldn't, maybe she would. Don't say
you will, don't say you won't, kind of thing. Or perhaps
the matter would be taken out of her hands. Maybe, by

8

the time the question came up – what with her being in his arms and not coming to any harm and everything – her knees would have gone so weak and trembly, and her tongue would have got so tied, all she would be able to do would be to nod weakly. Or not answer at all. And he might just kiss her fingertips anyway, without even asking.

It was enough to make you swoon, quite frankly.

The song came to an end. She pressed the repeat button and it began to replay. It was a great album, really, full of incredible tracks. But if she had to choose a favourite, it was *All Together In My Heart*, because as well as being a great song, Stevie took the lead vocals too. And if she had to choose a second favourite, it was *Remember Me One Night To Come*, which was so amazingly sad it made you cry every time you heard it. Made you weep complete buckets all over the place, like you were working for the fire brigade or something.

"Ally! What's the matter? What are you crying for?" her mum had demanded once, when she had walked into the room while the track was on. "What's the matter, girl? What's wrong? Is there trouble at school? Is someone picking on you? Are you not happy in your class? Try and tell us love, and we can maybe help to make it better."

But the words would barely come out. And when at last they did, all she could manage was, "Oh, Mum, Mum – it's so sad! So *sad!*"

"What is?" her mum said, looking around the room, perplexed.

"The song, Mum. *Remember Me One Night To Come.* Even though it isn't Stevie who sings the lead vocals on it. It's Bobby. But it's so sad, Mum, so sad."

"Is it?" Mum said. And for a moment it seemed as if she might say something a bit sarcastic, like: *If I'd spent all that money on a CD that sounded like that, I'd be sad as well.*

But she didn't. She just waited for Ally to go on.

"It's all about people who are in love, Mum. But they have to part, because it can never be."

"Why can it never be?" Mum said.

"It just can't, Mum. I don't know why. They don't say exactly in the song. They're not all that specific about it. But I think it's because their parents don't understand, and he's from the wrong part of town, and everyone says he's no good, and they're always putting him down. But it's not true that he's no good, Mum. It's just that no one understands him. Apart from her. And she can't see him any more, because they won't let her. And that's why it's sad."

But instead of making sarky remarks or funny cracks, Ally's mum said, "Put it on again. Let me hear it with you."

And Ally had, and her mum had sat on the bed next to her, and they had listened to Bobby singing *Remember*

Me One Night To Come in his rich, tender voice.

Mum stayed quiet all the way through, and when the song had finished and the last chorus of:

"Remember me one night to come
You always were the only one . . ."

had faded away, she looked at Ally and she said, "You know, Ally, that *is* sad. It is a good song, with a lovely tune. And they sang it really well."

And she didn't feel so bad then. She was glad her mum hadn't laughed. It made it all right. Like it wasn't odd or strange, and you didn't have to be a weirdo to cry at songs that made you sad.

When her mum had gone she played the song yet again, but she was careful to listen to it through the earphones, as maybe her mum might think that three listens and three cries in a row *was* a bit silly.

She realised then, as she listened to it for the third time, why it made her cry so much. It was her story. Their story. Hers and Stevie's. And it was sad because it would never be. She would never meet him, never know him, never not come to any harm in his arms, never need to make a decision as to whether he could kiss her fingertips or not.

"Remember me one night to come
You always were the only one."

But how could Stevie remember, when he had never

met her? There was nothing for him to remember. It was all down to her, to always remember him. And she would, of course, that went without saying. She would remember him until the day she died. And she would die a – what did they call them again? Oh yes, a spinster. She would never marry or anything, or love anyone else. She would become an old maid – a nun even. Because who was there to spend the rest of your life with if there wasn't Stevie? Stevie was the only one.

She played *All Together In My Heart* just once more before tea. And as reliable as an alarm clock that went off at the same time every morning, it wrung the same emotions from her heart. Her heart seemed to skip a beat or to beat too fast. And there it was, that weight again, that force lying on her, constricting her breathing, making it difficult to swallow, leaving her mouth dry and her throat tight. Crushing her.

"Remember me one night to come . . ."

Yes. That was all she could realistically expect, wasn't it? To see his poster on the ceiling above her. To see his picture in the pop magazines. To see him on TV and read about him in the fan club news. A disembodied voice, was all he would ever be.

"You always were the only one . . ."

And he would never know. Never know that she even existed. If only she could get to meet him – just once. See him. Talk to him. Touch him, even.

The door of her bedroom crashed open and her sister, Cheryl, burst in.

"Oi! Cloth-ears! We've been shouting for you for the past five minutes! Tea's ready. Couldn't you hear me yelling? Or have you gone deaf or something?"

Ally took her headphones off and stopped the CD.

"Sorry," she said. "I was just listening to something."

"Yeah," said Cheryl. "I can guess what, 'an all. So come on. Before it gets cold."

Cheryl went downstairs. Ally got up off her bed to follow. She turned for one last look at Stevie Manns, to sustain her through the meal: there he was. On his own. With the rest of the band. On stage. Standing by a pony in a field, chewing on a piece of grass. Walking along the seashore, looking sad and alone. Riding the dodgems at the fairground, laughing and looking happy. He didn't smoke or drink or take drugs. It said so in all the magazines. And fame and success hadn't gone to his head, not one bit at all. And he was just the same as he had been before, and still saw all his old friends.

She had twenty-five posters all together. Some sent off for, some cut out from magazines.

Ally hesitated for a moment in the doorway. Just say she was wrong. Just say it *was* possible to meet him. Just say it *could* be done. And why not? There *must* be a way, but how? Well, whatever the way was, she'd find it.

"Alice!" her mum's voice called up the stairs. "Your food's getting cold."

"Coming, Mum, coming!"

She closed the door behind her, leaving on the bedside light. Leaving it on – well, for Stevie, really.

Silly, yes. She knew.

Sort of like a shrine, really, as her dad said.

Yeah, yeah, yeah. She knew. She knew. She was sensible enough to know how daft she was being. But she left the light on for him just the same.

And maybe it was possible. Maybe it was possible at that.

She hurried down to the kitchen to join the rest of her family for tea. Not that she felt she could eat much. She was too excited. She was going to meet Stevie Manns.

Somehow, somewhere, and soon.

2

ABOUT THE STUFF

She had all the stuff, of course. All the stuff and the rest. And a good deal more on top.

First there was the just the ordinary stuff. Well, anyone could get that. You only needed to buy any one of a dozen magazines and you could get photos and centre spreads that turned into pin-ups – if you could prise the staples out without breaking your fingernails. You had to make sure that you didn't tear the page either as you went to take it out, or you'd rip Stevie's lovely smile in half or split Bobby R down the middle.

Stevie was the dreamy one, in some ways. Lovely face – but so sad, sometimes. And they said in the fanzine that some days he just wanted to get away from it all and to be alone. And Ally felt like that too on occasion. And Stevie would drive his Ferrari up on to the lonely moors and go for long walks, just like Heathcliff in that book they were supposed to be reading at school. *Wuthering Heights*, that was it. And there was that song about it, the one her mum had on a record. The Kate Bush one, where she went:

"Heathcliff, it's me I'm Catheeeee.

Woa oh oh oh . . ."

in a squeaky voice.

Where am I? What was I thinking about? Ally wondered.

You got so distracted, thinking about them. Your thoughts got all tangled up like washing in a machine.

Oh yeah. About where you got the stuff. Right.

Well, alongside the ordinary stuff that anybody could buy, there was also the official fan club stuff. You just had to send off a stamped addressed envelope for that and you got your membership card within twenty-one days, plus a full bumper pack of posters, special offers and priority booking forms for the concerts. And it was free – apart from the cost of the stamp. No, no catch. Absolutely free. Because that was what Stevie had always said, that they didn't want to rip the fans off, and it was the fans who mattered, and it was *their* club, and the Five Nine were *their* group. And he wanted everyone to know that.

In fact the band had even forced one man to drop his ticket prices, as he was overcharging. And he'd had to do it, or they wouldn't have played. Simple as that.

Fan club membership also meant that you could order special mixes of the singles. In fact there'd even been a fanzine mix of *Dance, Baby, Dance* (because they weren't just a ballads band, they could really rock things up as well) that you could only get mail order on quotation of your membership number, which made it totally exclusive to the real fans. There was personal information too, like profiles on individual band members: height, weight, age, likes, dislikes and so on. True, you could get that in the ordinary mags, but the fan club stuff was always a lot more intimate and behind the scenes.

And they always told you, too – in case you didn't know, like you'd been living on another planet for the past two years or something – about how the band got its name, the Five Nine. And about how Nitz got his name, which was quite funny really, and it wasn't what you'd have thought and had nothing to do with nits at all.

They told you why Bobby R never used his full name and why Charlie was always Charlie and no one ever called him anything else. And they said that when he had gone for his passport for the band's first international tour – when they were hoping to break into America which they hadn't yet, but they would one day soon – he had written his name down as Charlie. And the people at the passport office had said Charlie *who*? And he had said Charlie no one, just Charlie. Which had driven them wild, apparently, and was incredibly funny when you thought about it, and he was a tremendous joker with a great sense of humour, though a lot of people didn't appreciate that. And apparently a lot of them – like executives from the record company (*the suits*, as Bobby R called them in that interview he did a while back) – they just didn't get the joke. And they all stood about once Charlie got started, not knowing how to react. But if you were a fan, and you just sort of went with it (*go with the flow, bro*, as Charlie used to say) it was amazingly funny, really, especially as he delivered it all so totally straight, with this poker face all the time, and no one knew how to take him.

But it *was* funny. Sometimes in class Ally would be sitting there and she'd look up and catch the eye of her friend Pauline, a big Charlie fan, who sat at a desk just across the way. And she only had to say one word, or sometimes just do that Charlie look, with the one eyebrow raised and your mouth sort of scrumpled up – and that was *it!*

It was awful then, really, trying not to laugh like that. You felt you'd explode, and you sometimes did. You'd erupt with great giggling peals of laughter until Mrs Nary stopped the lesson and demanded an explanation of what was so funny.

But how could you explain? How could you explain to someone who was too old ever to understand? Mrs Nary, she was with the dinosaurs.

Some real hard-core Five Nine fans went to extraordinary lengths to see them or to get hold of souvenirs: things which the band members had actually used and had held in their very hands; old tissues they might have blown their noses on, T-shirts they had worn.

These die-hard fans would stand for hours outside the

band members' houses, hoping a chewing-gum wrapper would float down from an open window, or that they might actually look up and get a glimpse of their idols, while raking through their dustbins.

Not that you ever told your parents where you were going. Ally certainly didn't, the one time she went. She'd got the train one Saturday and had gone across town with Pauline – after first telling her mum that they were going to the Science Museum – to stand outside Stevie Manns's house in the hope that he might come to the window and give them a wave.

You didn't leave home in what you intended to arrive in, mind. No way. You left home in jeans and a sweat-shirt, and then stopped off on the way somewhere and got changed in a toilet cubicle into something a bit more eye-catching.

Because, let's face it, there was competition. And Stevie Manns wasn't even going to *see* you – let alone fall in love with you – if you were just one more face in a sea of faces, a wave in a tide of blue, one more foot-soldier in the denim army.

So a change of clothes in the backpack was absolutely essential and a load of make-up with you as well. Then, of course, it all had to be done the other way round before you got back home and every last trace of blusher and lipstick removed, or your mum might start getting suspicious.

"How was the Science Museum, love?"

"Great."

"Big queue to get in?"

"Not too bad."

"Pauline fine?"

"Great."

"She enjoy it too?"

"Yeah."

"You were there the *whole* afternoon then, were you? In the Science Museum? Didn't go *anywhere else*?"

"Yeah, Mum. The whole afternoon."

"Well, that's funny, because I had the radio on and they said they closed the Science Museum at one o'clock due to a bomb scare and they're still searching it now."

Gulp, double gulp, and gulp again.

Right in it that time, and no more trips up town with Pauline. Not for a long, long time.

The girls you met outside Stevie Manns's house though, some of them had all sorts of weird stuff. They treated these objects with bizarre reverence, as if they were relics from a crucifixion. Things like coke cans that Bobby R had actually drunk from. And occasionally they were even willing to sell them to you if the price was right.

Ally never went for any of that though. She was a fan, sure. A big fan. But she wasn't going to pay five pounds for an empty coke can just because some girl who was too young to wear eyeliner anyway told her that Bobby R had drunk from it and then passed it to Stevie, who'd given a swig to Charlie, who'd handed it to Nitz, who'd drained it to the dregs and then thrown it into the crowd. And Miss Itsy-Bitsy Mini Skirt here, who looked like a bad case of anorexia anyway, had happened to catch it as it fell.

Because how did you *know*? How did you know she wasn't just trying to make a quick fiver? It could have been her own coke can, or she might have filched it from a recycling bin.

No way, matey. No thank you. Pull the other one, it's got Pepsi on!

They had seen him though, her and Pauline. At least they'd thought it was him. A face at an upstairs window. A faint smile. A wave.

"Stevie, Stevie!"

A major hearts-fluttering situation.

Or maybe it wasn't him at all. Just a roadie or someone, pretending to be him. They all did that, didn't they? Right old load of swank. Anyone connected with the band all trying to be important. Anyone who came in or went out. Making out they were like personal friends or something, when they'd probably only just called round to fix a washer on the tap.

Stevie moved house every now and again, when the attention got too much. But the hard-core fans traded addresses and ex-directory phone numbers, and within a couple of weeks the watchers and the waiters were back at the door.

He had another house too, out in the country – or so the rumour said.

"Mum, me and Pauline thought we'd like to go out to the country this Saturday. It's nature study. For our project at school. Is that okay?"

Her mum had eased up by then over the Science Museum business and she let Ally go. Though it was all sensible shoes and *take your anorak and be sure to phone as soon as you get there*, and all that kind of stuff.

They'd spent an hour and a half on the bus and another hour after that, tramping over wet and sodden fields, trying to find Stevie's secret cottage retreat where he liked to go to be alone and to commune with nature and to try and write the lyrics for the next album. But all they'd got was soaked.

Now why was Stevie writing lyrics, when he was more of a singer than a songwriter?

Well, the thing was that because Bobby R wrote most of the songs and had written *all* of the hit singles, he made a lot more money than the other three members of the band.

This had apparently caused some friction, and it didn't seem exactly fair that Bobby R should be making so much more than the others when they had all contributed equally to their success. Except, of course that he *had* written the songs. But in fairness, it's how you sing and play them that counts too.

So Bobby and the rest had agreed that they would all write the songs for the next album, and so Stevie was trying to write his share. But as he had said back in that fanzine interview in February, "I'm a lover, not a fighter, and a singer, not a writer." Which was quite sort of witty really, when you thought about it.

Not like Nitz though. Nitz *was* a fighter.

Nitz was a bit frightening, really.

You wouldn't want to go and stand outside Nitz's house. He'd probably open the window and invite you in.

And then what would you do? Would you go in or what?

Well, some girls would, Ally knew that. Some girls definitely would. There were girls in her class at school who thought Nitz was just gorgeous. And one of them, Margie Saunders, had even lied about her age and gone and had a tattoo, just like Nitz's, done on her arm.

Margie's mum had gone wild. Like Tarzan! Positively swinging from the branches! Though the man who'd done the tattoo swore on his granny's tattooed grave that he'd thought Margie Saunders was over eighteen. So you can imagine what she must have been wearing for him to believe that, and it certainly wasn't her old Brownies uniform.

Margie's mum kicked up no end of a stink and she even went to the newspapers about it and it was soon on the TV as well. Major outcry, it was. Major tattooing scandal and the end of civilisation as we know it.

Schoolgirl Gets Tattoo To Be Like Pop Idol! the headlines said. Then they tried to blame it all on Nitz, for ever having a tattoo in the first place. Like it was a crime to have a tattoo. And all these smarmy MPs were lining up to say what a disgrace it was, as if wearing a suit like they did made you an honest person or something. But what about *them*, going about with their hands in the till all the time? What about that?

Anyway, a lot of girls were jealous, as Margie Saunders got her photo in the paper and became a *cause for concern* and a *story of our times*. She was even invited on to Kilroy-Silk with her mum and dad to have the whole thing out in front of the cameras. Some people at school carried on as if Margie had planned it all deliberately, just to get attention. Of course, there were girls at school who *would* have done it for that reason. People like that were always having problems and going round being really pathetic and all mysterious in the hope that somebody would notice and ask them what was wrong.

Ally hated all that, all that putting it on and being pathetic. She loved Stevie Manns and knew that if she could ever get to meet him, he would love her too. She

24

even had a good idea of how many babies they would have. But she wasn't going to go all girly and pathetic about it. What was the point of that? You couldn't see Stevie Manns getting all lovey-dovey about someone who'd gone all pathetic.

Stupid.

Still, maybe some girls couldn't help it. It was a difficult age, after all, so her mum told her.

"Growing up," she said, "is difficult."

To which her dad had added, "Yeah, and being born is difficult, and being middle-aged is difficult and being old is difficult, and being dead is probably pretty difficult as well. In fact, if there's any time of life that's an easy one, I've yet to find it."

He went back to his paper then, like he'd had a bad day, but no one had bothered to ask him about it. He probably wanted a bit of attention really. Sort of *I've got a hard life too, you know* kind of thing.

Gone a bit pathetic, really, in his own way.

Where was she now?

Your mind went everywhere, flitting and scudding about. *Butterfly mind*, Mrs Nary had said. *Bee mind*, Ally had thought, because she always tried to take a little pollen and a little nectar away with her from whatever flowers she stopped at.

Oh yeah, anyway, Margie Saunders. So in the end she had the tattoo removed by laser treatment on the

National Health. And she was lucky to get it too, apparently, and she'd only jumped to the top of the waiting list because of her age.

There was something else too, which Ally kept thinking about. Something which kept coming back into her mind, no matter how many times she tried to push the thoughts away from her. It was all that stuff the papers wrote about Stevie and that supermodel, Caslile. Well, sure, it was obvious he was going to go out with someone like her, he was a pop star, and they always went out with models. But to say it was serious and to make out they were in love and stuff, well, that was just to sell newspapers. Ally didn't believe it, not for a second. Caslile wasn't Stevie's type. You could tell Caslile wasn't his type. And what sort of a stupid name was that anyway? Because nobody in the entire world had ever been christened *Caslile*. She'd obviously made the whole thing up for a bit of flash; to try and impress people, so that all the magazines and clothes designers and what-have-you would ring up the model agency and say, "We must have Caslile for our winter collection," and "We must have Caslile for the next shoot."

But if she'd gone about operating under her own name, which was probably something like Gladys Snurkle or something, she'd never have worked again. Because who'd ever ring up and say, "We must have Gladys Snurkle for the front cover of Vogue!"

Do me a favour!

Ally and Pauline had a pretty good laugh about that. Caslile – alias Gladys Snurkle. And they made a name up for that girl Charlie was seen with at Stringfellow's nightclub too, that artist called Rowenita Strong, and they said her real name was probably Whata Pong, and that her paintings stank almost as much as she did.

But these girls weren't Stevie's type, not really, you just knew. Or thought you did. You had a feeling. And Ally felt that she knew exactly what Stevie's type would be.

His type would sort of look like Ally – just a bit.

Her bedroom swam back into focus. Stevie Manns looked down at her from the posters. Now what *had* she been thinking? Something really important. Oh yes, that she'd never been to a Five Nine concert, that was it. Never seen them live and in the flesh. And it was her birthday soon and she was entitled to a treat. Her mum was going to ask her what she wanted: whether she wanted a party at the skating rink like last year or maybe a trip to a theme park.

But now Ally knew precisely what she was going to ask for. She knew just where she wanted to go.

There was no doubt at all in her mind.

3

THE TREAT

Plans and schemes. Hopes and dreams. What was it they said when you were a kid? Oh yeah. *If wishes were horses, then beggars would ride.*

Needed a bit of updating, that, now. *If wishes were lucky numbers then we'd all win the lottery.* How's that?

If wishes came true though.

If wishes came true.

"If wishes came true, what?"

Pauline was looking at her. They had been walking home together from school and had stopped on the bridge over the canal, as they often did, to look down into the water.

"What?" Ally said. She must have been dreaming again.

"You said, 'If wishes came true'."

"Did I?"

"Yeah. And then you stopped."

"I must have been thinking out loud."

"So what were you thinking out loud?"

"I was thinking that if wishes came true, I'd get to go to the Five Nine concert in Birmingham and I'd get to meet Stevie and get to talk to him – maybe dance with him—"

"*Snog* with him," Pauline suggested.

"*Pauline!*"

Ally felt herself colour. Pauline was all right and a good friend in her way. (Although she was obviously misguided, being such a Charlie fan rather than a Stevie fan, which told you a lot in itself.) But she didn't half come out with some stuff!

"Well, you do want to, don't you?"

"No, I don't."

"Yes, you do. Of course you do. Snogging is what it's all about."

She was always bringing things down a bit was Pauline, to a sort of – well – crude level.

Not that Ally was afraid to stand up for herself.

"Look, Pauline," she said. "It's *love* I'm talking about. True and pure and forever. That's how I feel about Stevie. *Love.*"

"Well, sure," Pauline agreed. "I'm not saying otherwise. But snogging comes into it too, doesn't it?"

"Not at all," Ally told her. "Me and Stevie are above snogging. Ours is a higher kind of love."

"Nobody's above snogging," Pauline said. "I bet you want to snog him really."

Ally looked at her pityingly. "The difference between you and me, Pauline," she said, "is that I'm a romantic."

"The difference between you and me, Ally," Pauline told her, "is that you're not being honest."

They dropped the subject and looked down into the dirty water of the canal.

"Look at all that Muck," Pauline said. "Isn't half muddy, eh?"

"Yes – Muddy Waters," Ally said. "Isn't that a song? I'm sure my dad's got it on a CD. It sound like an old bloke in pain.

"It's the blues," Pauline said. "The blues always sounds like old blokes in pain. My dad's got that sort of stuff, too. Only I thought Muddy Waters was a singer, not a song."

"Maybe he's both? Perhaps he sings about himself."

A narrow canal boat passed under the bridge.

"If my little brother was here, he'd try and spit down the funnel," Pauline said.

"Disgusting," Ally said. "And childish."

"Boys are."

"Not Stevie and Charlie though."

"They're men."

"*Real* men."

"I bet they wouldn't go gobbing down boats' funnels as they passed under bridges," Pauline said.

"Nitz would," Ally told her.

"He is *wild!*"

"Wild!"

"*Totally* wild."

"Mad!"

"What about Bobby R?" Pauline asked.

"I don't know about him. He'd be on the boat, probably. Or he'd write a song about it."

"About people spitting down funnels?"

"No. About being on the boat and the meaning of it all. You know, about how you pass by and never settle down and are always travelling or something."

"Do you think anyone actually fancies Bobby R though?" Pauline said. She offered Ally a piece of sugar-free chewing gum. "I mean, I know he writes the songs, but when they're up on stage, he's a bit buried in the screaming, really."

"What do you mean?"

"I mean everyone's screaming and he's preening about, but do you actually know anyone who screams for *him*?"

"No," Ally admitted. "I can't think of anyone. But there must be somebody."

Pauline thought a moment. "His mum, probably," she said. "She screams for him. She screams 'Where the hell have you been, Bobby? You only went out for a pint of milk. Not to be a pop star.'"

Ally laughed.

"They are men though," Pauline said. "At least compared to that lot at school. Bunch of wimps they are, half of them. All spots and acne."

"Yes, the Five Nine are real men," Ally agreed, as if she was a connoisseur. "How old do you think they are?"

She knew the answer, because it was in the fan club magazine. But it was nice to talk about it and to speculate.

"Well, Charlie's got to be eighteen." Pauline said. "And Stevie can't be far behind him. Anyway, it's in the Facts And Info bit."

"I don't believe all of that," Ally said. "Not always. They tell you lies and what they want you to believe. I bet there's things they don't tell us, secrets and that."

They looked down into the water again. The mud was settling back down where the boat had stirred it up.

"Do you think it matters," Ally said, "the age gap between us and them?"

Pauline thought.

"No," she said. "Why should it make a difference?"

"I've read," Ally said, "that relationships can flounder when the age gap is too wide." It had been an article in one of her mother's magazines, titled *Too Young, Too Old, Too Far Apart?* And there had been some real life case histories in it too, where only the names had been changed.

"No," said Pauline, "I wouldn't worry about it. It's only a few years. And girls mature before boys. We're probably as grown up as they are. And besides, I look at it this way: when Charlie is ninety, I'll be in my mid-eighties. Doesn't seem such a difference then, does it?"

"No, it doesn't, not when you put it like that."

The water was quite still again. Like a brown, muddy mirror.

"Well, go on then, if you're going," Pauline said, looking down into it. "I can't stand here all day. I have got a home to go to and homework to do when I get there."

"All right."

Alice took a pound coin from the pocket of her coat. She held it between finger and thumb, closed her eyes and made her wish.

"Are you sure you want to use a pound?" Pauline said. "It's a lot of money. You could borrow this two pence piece instead, if you like, and give it us back later."

"No," Ally said. "It has to cost. You have to make sacrifices. You have to pay the price for dreams to come true."

She kissed the coin, squeezed it tightly in her fist, then held her hand out over the parapet of the bridge.

"You sure it's lucky, the canal?" Pauline said. "I mean, are you sure wishes come true here?"

Ally turned and looked at her. Pauline could be so negative at times.

"Well, there's nowhere else round here, is there?"

"There's the fountain in the shopping mall," Pauline said. "People are always bunging their loose change in there and making wishes."

"That's not real, that's artificial," Ally said. "And it all goes to charity anyway."

"What's wrong with that?"

"Nothing. But it's not real. It's charity. It's not wrong. It's just not real wishes. You can't just make a well or a fountain and say 'Here you are, it's a wishing well,' all of a sudden. Something has to happen. It has to come about. It has to have a bit of mystery or some history. People need to have come and gone."

"So why's the canal lucky?" Pauline wanted to know.

"Because . . ." Ally said, and she dropped the coin into the muddy water, praying under her breath that her wish might come true.

"Because what?"

Ally picked up her bag. It was done. The wish was made.

"Because – it's old, and full of memories and also because – oh, nothing."

"Come on. Because *what*?"

Ally coloured. She wasn't going to say at first. But then . . .

"This is where my mum and dad met."

"What, in the canal?" Pauline said. "Didn't they get wet?"

"They met on the bridge. You know what I mean. Well, not met, exactly. But they used to come here, my mum said, when they were young and had no money.

And my mum threw a pebble in and made a wish."

"What wish?"

"That she and Dad would get married."

"And did they?"

"Get lost, Pauline."

"I'm only joking. No, it's romantic. Go on."

"And she wished that they'd be happy."

"And are they?"

"I think so."

"What, despite having you and Cheryl to make their lives a misery?"

"We were part of the wish, Mum said."

"Two girls?"

"Well, a boy and a girl."

"Didn't quite come true then?"

"You can't expect it all to come true. Not *all* of it."

"Can't you?"

"No. I don't think so. Just some of it. The best bits."

"Like if you met him. Touched him. Held his hand. *Snogged* him."

"Are we going home, Pauline, or what?"

"Well, tell me then, what did you wish?"

"I can't tell, can I? Or it won't come true. And anyway, you know."

"And did you wish for me as well?"

"Can't you wish for yourself?"

"Not at a quid a go, I can't. I haven't got the money."

"All right, hang on." Ally closed her eyes and added a PS to her wish, wishing for Pauline too. "Right, done."

"Thanks."

They stood a moment longer, looking down into the water.

"I'm so in love with him, Pauline," Ally said. "So in love it hurts. It hurts when I think of him and it hurts when I don't. It just hurts all the time. And yet I'd rather suffer it than not be in love at all."

"I know," Pauline said. "I know. I feel the same about Charlie, I think."

They went on their way, walking without speaking, going along the canal bank then turning off and cutting across the playing fields.

After a while, Ally began to hum a tune softly to herself and then to sing:

"All together in my heart
You'll see we two will never part . . ."

And then Pauline joined in, going:

"Chuggy-chug-chuggy
Chag a woo-ahh!"

By the time they got to the shopping precinct, they were singing so loudly that people were staring. And not only singing, they were doing the whole dance routine too. In fact, they did the whole thing so well, they even got a round of applause from some workmen on a building site, and there were shouts of, "Encore, en-core!"

They blushed and laughed and hurried on their way, giggling. They split up at the corner of Burnthouse Road and went towards their homes.

"Hope it comes true," Pauline yelled. "Keep them crossed!" And she held two crossed fingers up and then walked off humming *Never Believe Those Lies* to herself as she went.

Wishes. If wishes were riches. If wishes came true. If only it could be. If only she could make it happen. If only.

Ally's fast walk turned into a jog. She met Cheryl, who was coming the other way along the street, all dressed up to the nines.

"Hey, dream-head, what's the rush?"

"Cheryl, where are you going?"

She waved a letter at her.

"Post office."

Only *Cheryl* would get dressed up like that just to go to the post office. And why? Well, Ally could tell you why. Because she might run into Michael Lawrence on the way, that was why. All that effort, just for a bloke. And not ashamed of it or anything.

Roll on the feminist revolution. Or come back and try again, more like. It seemed to have passed Cheryl by, gone right over her head and left her unaffected, –

without even minor injuries – and hardly liberated at all.

Her sister went on her way. Ally looked back to see that Cheryl's bum was wiggling again. She surely must be helping it to do that. It definitely didn't have to wiggle that much. She must be doing something to it. She was leading it into bad habits, that's what she was doing. What an embarrassment. She'd get a rosette, if she carried on like that, for being the biggest embarrassment in the neighbourhood. She'd win first prize and special mentions, plus a year's supply of wiggles and a cup for the mantelpiece.

Ally's jog turned into a run. She went up the path, round the back, and into the kitchen. She shut the door behind her firmly, not meaning to slam it. Her mum looked up from the potatoes.

"Where's the fire?" she said. "Have you come to put it out?"

"Mum," Ally said, "Mum, I know what I want for my birthday. For my big birthday treat, like you said."

"Oh yes. You've decided, have you?"

"Yes, Mum."

"A few friends round to the skating rink again then, is it? Or would you like to try the ten pin bowling this year?"

"Mum, I want to go to a concert."

"A concert? What sort of concert?"

"A pop concert. I want to see the Five Nine, Mum. They're playing a gig – on my *birthday*. Can I go, Mum, and take Pauline. Can I? *Can I?*"

Her mum put down the knife she had been using to cut the potatoes.

"Well, I don't know," she said. "I don't know about that at all. I think we'll need to talk it over."

4

THE FIVE NINE

All right then, so why the Five Nine?

Well, how many different explanations have you got time for? If there was just the one, it would be easy, but what's ever that simple?

The Five Nine, then; the reason and the cause.

Okay, so here goes.

Right. Well, the first explanation is the most obvious one, and it's probably the one that's true. It's also the officially approved version in the fan club magazine and it goes like this.

Now, Bobby R is forming the band—

Okay, qualify that instantly. Bobby R *says* he formed the band. Charlie says *he* formed the band. And they argue about it sometimes. But it's just in fun. Okay. So we all know that, and we don't need to get into that argument again right now and open up that particular can of worms.

Okay. So Bobby R – or Charlie or whoever, but *someone* – formed the band, and it gets to be so that there's three of them in it at that time Bobby R, Charlie and Nitz.

They'd all just left school then, and they'd none of them got jobs, and by the look of it there weren't going to be any jobs. Not that they didn't have exam passes, they did. But Bobby R wanted to be a songwriter, and he wasn't even looking for a job because he was really single-minded and just focused on this one thing. And Charlie couldn't find a job, not even with a magnifying glass, no matter how hard he looked. And as for Nitz, well, he might be a fantastic drummer but let's face it, baby, is he unemployable! With a capital U! Because, honestly, could you see anyone behind a bank counter looking like *that*? Tattoos, studs, earrings and that hair! Not really somehow. So he was right out of the running in the collar-and-tie-and-job-with-a-pension stakes.

So anyway, there they are. They've got the song-writing talent and keyboard player, the drummer and the bass guitar. So what they need now is someone with a voice and looks and stage presence, and with something else – star quality.

So they audition a few would-bees, wanna-bees, could-bees and me-me-mees, but none of them are right.

Then they think of Stevie Manns, who went to a different school from the rest of them, but who once used to live in the same street as Bobby R, and Bobby remembers him from when they were both in the Sunday school choir. He wonders if Stevie's still got a voice. Which Stevie has, even if it's a bit deeper by now – and he isn't wearing short trousers any more.

I mean, can you imagine Stevie, a choir boy, in short trousers?

Hoot!

So Bobby R goes to see Stevie and they have a sort of try-out and stuff, and fool around on the guitar, and then they formally ask him if he'd like to be in the band. Because by then, Bobby R has played him some of his songs on the keyboards, and he's met Charlie and Nitz, and so he knows what he's getting into. And he can see that they aren't just another bunch of time-wasters, but three really talented guys.

Only the thing is, Stevie-wise, that Stevie *does* have a job. With this very good firm, and they really like him and think he'll go far, all the way to the top. He's beaten loads of other applicants to get this job too, and he's only been there three months or so into the bargain. So he's got quite a lot to lose.

So there Stevie is, with a job and a future. And here are these three other guys with nothing but hopes and dreams and a handful of songs, and that's all. No record company interest, no recording deals, no manager, no Mr Ten Percent, no gigs lined up, nothing. Bobby R knows a guy called Dave Marks, who has a second-hand record and CD stall at the market – rarities and deletions – and who also has part shares in the

Department Of Hope, a sort of nightclub, rave-den kind of place. And he puts on gigs in the summer, sometimes, out in the country. Anyway, he's interested in getting into management, if the right group ever comes along. But it hasn't. At least not yet.

So they send Stevie his call-up papers and formally ask him to join the band. It's yes-or-no time, and if he doesn't take it, they have to find someone else. But does he want to be in the army, or is he going to dodge the draft?

At first Stevie says, "Okay, well look, let's do it as a part-time thing. Evenings and weekends. Then if it takes off, fine. If it doesn't nobody's lost anything. I like the band. The songs sound great. Sure, I'd like to be in it. But to make it a full-time thing straightaway would be a mistake."

Charlie and Nitz think this is okay and reasonable. But not Bobby R.

So Bobby R says, "No way. No half measures. It's all or nothing."

He wants absolute commitment. This is a full-time, all-day thing. Promotion, hustling, learning and arranging the songs, working on the dance routines. This is serious. Not just another garage band kind of thing. Not just another bunch of kids who play a few chords and do a few gigs and who are never heard of again.

He wants total dedication. Full-time. No other way.

Stevie isn't so sure now. It's easier for the others.

What have they got to lose? But Stevie has a job and a future and a career to go down the tubes. And those things don't come your way so often. So he says, "Okay, two questions. One, what about the job I have? And two, what the hell's this band called?"

They haven't really discussed that point, so Bobby R says, "Look, Stevie, we know you'll be quitting your job and taking a big risk. We know that. But think of the future. If this works out, it's got to be better than the nine to five." And then as an afterthought he adds, "Oh, and by the way, that's the name of the band, the Five Nine. Because it's better than the nine to five!"

Right off the top of his head.

And the name stuck, and there it is, and the rest is history and geography and one huge pile of newspaper cuttings and one big warehouse of album sales and a million decibels of screaming fans.

Other explanations doing the rounds. (And the best way to take them is with the biggest pinch of salt you can find.)

1. Stevie once lived at a house with the number fifty-nine on the door. (Not true. He lived at number forty-three.)

2. Charlie was born on the fifth of September. The fifth day of the ninth month. (Not true either. He was born on November eighth. It was his *sister* who was born on September the fifth.)

3. Nitz was born on the ninth of May. The ninth day of the fifth month. Turn it around and you get five and nine again. (Another nice try, but not true either. Nitz is a Leo. Not a Capricorn, and has all the typical characteristics. Though whether you believe in that is up to you.)

4. Bobby R was flipping a coin, attempting to decide on whether to give up songwriting and try to get on to a City and Guilds course or not. The coin wouldn't land the way he wanted, so he kept on flipping it until he got the best five out of nine calls. (Complete fiction. Bobby never thought of giving up songwriting. Ever.)

5. Five and nine are Nitz's lucky numbers. (Absolute garbage. Nitz doesn't even have a lucky number. He has a lucky *colour*. Not a number. Call yourself a fan? Well, try again, dunce!)

These are the most common theories and there must be a hundred more like them. But the reality is that it all just happened. It came right off the wall. It just came down the chimney like a Christmas present.

But no doubt you'll believe what you want to believe, and that's up to you. These kinds of rumours and stories are like buses, anyway, there's always going to be another one along in a minute.

So if it's going your way, you take it – if that's where you want to be.

5

ENEMY NO. 1

"It's what I want Mum. Really. It's *definitely* what I want. Please! I'll never ask for another birthday present ever again . . . at least not until next year anyway!"

"Okay, Ally. I've no objection in principle. Find out how much the tickets are and we'll see what we can do."

"Okay. Great, Mum. Thanks!"

And Ally went off to use the phone.

Being an official Five Nine fan meant that you had priority on the tickets for the gigs. You rang up, quoted your membership number, and not only did you have choice of the seats, you got a discount too.

And − (*are you listening?*) − your name went automatically into a draw. And if you won, you got a *back stage pass* to meet the band *in person* after the show, *and* you got invited to the party afterwards.

There was always a party, after every gig. Because the band were just so up, there was no way they could sleep after all that. They just had to go on dancing, talking, listening to music, until they wound down enough to be able to crash out at four or five in the morning.

Ally rang the fan club booking service using the phone in the living room. She got the recorded *you are in a queue, do not hang up, your call will soon be dealt with* for a few minutes, then there was a click, and another voice.

"Hello. Five Nine Fan Club Ticket Hot Line. Can I help?"

"Hello, yes. This is Ally – Alice Morgan. Oh, did you want my membership number?"

"Do you want to tell me what the enquiry is first?"

"Er, yeah. I was ringing to ask, actually, if you still have any tickets for the concert next month on the twenty-ninth."

"In Birmingham?"

"Yes."

"At the National Exhibition Centre?"

"Yeah."

"Yes, we still have a few tickets left for fan club members, but you'll need to be quick, they're going fast."

"Right, okay. I'll have to get back to you. Only how much are they, as a matter of fact?"

"Fifteen pounds."

"Each?"

"Yes."

Each. Why had she said that? She knew they were fifteen pounds each. What else would they be. Stupid

47

thing to say. Why did she say stupid things even when she knew they were stupid? Nerves probably.

Anyway, was that it? Was that all she needed to know?

No, couple of other things.

"Actually, I live quite near London," Ally said. "There're no tickets left for the London dates I suppose?"

"No, sorry love. Not one. I mean, you could chance going there and getting one from the scalpers."

"The who?"

"Ticket touts. But I wouldn't risk it. They'd rip you off. And they might be forged anyway. And I'm sure as a fan club member, you'd know how Stevie and Bobby feel about ticket touts."

They didn't like the fans being ripped off. No two ways about that.

"Do you want to book for Birmingham then, love?"

"Probably. I will do," Ally said. "Just have to check. What'll I need to book them?"

"A credit card number?"

Credit card number! She'd be lucky. Pocket money number, maybe, and that certainly didn't run into six digits.

"I'll have to get back to you."

"Well, I wouldn't leave it too long."

"You can't hold them for me?"

"Sorry. Not without a credit card number. And as I

48

say, I wouldn't be too long. They're going like hot cakes."

It was always hot cakes, wasn't it, Ally thought. That was what things always went like, hot cakes. Never cold coconuts, or lukewarm lemonade. Yet the funny thing was that Ally had never in her life seen hot cakes going like hot cakes anywhere. Who had ever seen people queuing up for hot cakes?

"Hello, caller. Are you still there?"

The voice broke into her thoughts. Must happen all the time. Must get a lot of dreamers on the Five Nine Ticket Hot Line. Dreaming of Stevie or Bobby R or . . .

"Yes, I'm still here, thanks. I'll get back to you."

"Well, as I say, don't leave it too late or the tickets will all be gone."

"I won't. I'll get right back. Thanks. Bye."

Ally hung up and went in search of her mum. She felt pretty confident about it. She was sure her mum would wear fifteen quid. She might even wear the thirty and pay for Pauline as well. After all, what good was a birthday treat without a friend to share it with.

Me and my friend

Na, na, nee, na, na!

For some reason the taunting voice of Marlene Forrester came into her mind.

Ah, get lost, Marlene Go away!

Everyone should have a Marlene Forrester in their

life. Then own personalised, monogrammed, made-to-measure Marlene Forrester with customised number-plates. A bit like a bullet with your name on. Marlene Forrester. Everyone should have an enemy, if only once in their lives, just for the sake of experience. Just to know what it feels like to be a persecuted minority. It helps you understand a lot of things, like wars and history and why people end up on murder charges.

Say the gruesome words, Marlene Forrester, and then wash your mouth out with soap.

It was funny that such a dislike should have developed between them. It was hard to tell when or why it had started. She and Marlene had known each other for years – since primary school. For years they'd managed to ignore each other; never a crossed line, a crossed word or a crossed path.

And maybe that was it. That was the cause of it. Now their paths *had* crossed, and they seemed to have run headlong right smack bang into each other and were still reeling from the impact.

For years they'd co-existed, like hostile powers on a common border. Only maybe they weren't hostile back then. They'd even invited each other to their birthday parties, back when they were small.

"Are you going to invite Marlene, Ally? She did ask you to hers," her mum would remind her.

"Yeah, all right. I suppose."

50

And she did invite her. Had to really. And Marlene normally brought quite a decent present with her too, though you knew that her mum had paid for it.

After those early days, there were years of indifference between them. They lived very close to each other. Their houses were in different streets, but their rear gardens both bordered Hammerston Park. When they looked out of their bedrooms, they could see the backs of each other's houses. At least they could in the winter, when the trees were bare.

Their mothers were always trying to push them together. And you could see why, too. If they'd been as tight as two fleas, then it would have made a lot of things easier. Mum could have left Ally round at Mrs Forrester's house, and Mrs Forrester could have left Marlene round at their house.

But it never did quite work out like that. And now, after years of nodding acquaintance, suddenly, from out of the blue, they were sworn enemies.

It seemed to happen when Marlene went fashionable.

She'd never been trendy before. But she must have got self-conscious one day and so she went and bought all this stuff to totter around in, which her mum must have paid for. She looked like a right dog's dinner in it too, and she even got sent home from school once for being outrageous.

"Dress codes are dress codes," Mr Bute the headmaster had said. "And I will not have them contravened."

And there everyone is, hunting for dictionaries, to look *contravened* up. And all it meant was breaking the rules, and why couldn't he have said that in the first place?

"School is a place for learning. Not a place for making fashion statements. If you wish to make those, you must do so in your own time."

Not that the way Marlene Forrester looked was exactly a fashion statement. More of a fashion question mark. Or a fashion disaster.

So anyway, it was round about then that it all started.

"Probably her hormones," Pauline had said. "Can't handle them. A lot of girls get like that at her age." (Her age was their age too, but somehow that was different).

"Yeah, hormones come over them," Pauline went on knowledgeably, "and they don't know what to do. It all gets horribly hormones and they go a bit do-lally. Dressing up all funny, or spending half their lives posing in front of the mirror with nothing but their undies on and wondering if they'll ever have a boyfriend."

Ally did wonder if Pauline wasn't speaking from experience.

"One moment they think they're beautiful," Pauline went on, "and the next, they think they're the ugliest thing since squashed cow-pats. It's sort of identity crisis, that's what it is. It's all psychology."

"How," Ally asked her, "do you know?"

"I've been there," Pauline admitted, without a trace of shame. "Been there, done that, lived through it and survived. Yeah, I'm a hormone survivor. I've come out of the other end of the tunnel, more or less unscathed."

"Me too," Alice lied, feeling that far from coming out of the tunnel she wasn't even halfway along it, and that a train might come along and flatten her at any time. She suspected that Pauline was lying too, and that she was also still in the tunnel herself.

"We should start up a Hormone Survivors' Group," Pauline said. "Set up a hot line, you know. We could call it the Hormone Crisis Centre. Girls in distress could ring us up for advice, to discuss things they feel they can't mention to their parents. We might even get a grant from the council."

But whatever it was – a genuine hormone crisis or trouble at home or just a sudden and simple clash of personalities – it soon became clear that this neighbourhood, this school, this town, possibly even this universe, wasn't quite big enough for both Marlene and Ally.

For just as there was chalk and cheese, there was Marlene Forrester and there was Ally Morgan.

At first it was just little digs. And *she* started it. Didn't she? Well, it seemed that way. Ally searched her memory, trying to think of anything she herself could have done to offend or to provoke her. Some inadvertent slight or unthinking rudenesses? Had she bumped against Marlene in the corridor? Knocked her drink over in the dining-hall? Elbowed her at netball? She couldn't remember.

Little digs and then bigger ones. Sarcasm at first.

"That's a nice coat, Alice Morgan," she had said, one morning.

"Oh thanks."

"Yes, I really like that coat. Don't you, Tracey?"

And of course Marlene had her friends too. Which was another part of the mystery. How come *they* had friends. The people who were so nasty and unpleasant to you? How come they still had friends? How come everyone didn't see right through Marlene, see how transparent and malicious she was? Were Marlene's friends as nasty as she was? How come anyone could like her?

Yes, how come?

So anyway. Little digs at first, then bigger digs, and then great bulldozer-sized digs started appearing in Ally's life, like she was being got at by a JCB. It was out-and-out war by then. Just peace one moment, a few short rumblings of discontent, and then total and absolute war the next.

Ally did her best to fight back, while she tried to work

out what had happened. No Marlene Forrester or any-one was going to make her life unhappy. And if she as much as laid one finger . . .

But she didn't. Maybe she was scared to. Or a bit too clever. Because Ally was bigger and stronger. So it wasn't like that. And yet in some ways it was as bad, if not worse.

After all, how could you go up to someone and say, "Marlene Forrester's picking on me," when Marlene Forrester only just came up to your shoulder?

But for all that, it was a kind of bullying just the same. Mental bullying. No bruises, no visible scars; just endless jibes and sneers and sniggers behind your back. And sudden footprints appearing on your maths homework when you popped out of the class for a moment.

If Marlene had had more people on her side, it would have been worse. Maybe even intolerable. She had certainly tried to whip up public feeling against Ally on more than one occasion to turn the rest of the class against her. But she had failed.

People liked Ally. She wasn't Miss Popular Personality and Pom Poms of the year or anything. They just liked her, in an ordinary sort of way. Or rather, they didn't dislike her. She got on with them. She had her friends and her special friends, and the rest were just acquain-tances who didn't care too much one way or the other. But they weren't enemies, and for all that Marlene tried, she couldn't turn them into enemies either. Not even Tracey entirely. Tracey was Marlene's friend and so she seemed to go along with it when they were together. But if ever Ally met Tracey on her own, she was fine, quite chatty, perfectly all right.

So all right that Ally had once said to her during the school lunch hour, "What's this all about then? With you and Marlene and the snide remarks all the time?"

"What do you mean?" Tracey had said, all innocence, as if a Cornetto wouldn't melt in her mouth.

"*You* know, Tracey."

"Oh, *that*. It's just Marlene. I don't know."

"Yeah, but I mean, what did I do to upset her? Did I stand on her pet spider or something?"

"I don't know," Tracey said, a bit shiftily. But Ally knew that she *did* know. She just wasn't telling.

"Well, maybe you could tell her to pack it in."

"I can't tell her to pack something in when she's not even doing anything, Ally."

She looked at Ally a bit slyly then. The way she sometimes did when she was backing Marlene up.

And then Ally finally got the truth.

Just as Tracey was going, she fired the parting shot.

"You're a big Five Nine fan, aren't you, Ally?"

"Yeah, so?"

"Nothing." She walked on a step, then paused and looked back. "Marlene's a big Five Nine fan too."

"So? It's a free country."

"Who's your favourite though?"

For a second she wasn't going to tell. But then, why not?

"Stevie," Ally said, almost defiantly, as if she'd just come out of some kind of closet or other and gone public. "Stevie's my favourite. He's the best."

"Yeah, well Marlene's a big Stevie fan too," Tracey told her. "She even says she *loves* him!"

And having fired the last of her ammunition, Tracey went off to join Marlene on the other side of the playground.

The last thing Ally had heard before the bell went was Marlene saying, "What were you talking to *her* for!" And Tracey said, "Oh, nothing." And then it was time to go back in.

Still, at least she had some kind of an explanation now. Ridiculous in many ways though it was. But at least she could begin to shape things into some kind of sense.

They were rivals. Rivals for Stevie's love. And on Marlene's side, it was plainly a bitter, jealous, vindictive rivalry. Hence the jibes and the sarcasm and the footprint on the maths book that had suddenly appeared from nowhere.

And what about the phone calls? The funny ones to the house? Like the time the taxi came round and nobody had ordered one. And then an undertaker turned up at the door, looking all sad and solemn and asking should he come in and measure up?

"There's no one dead here," her mum had said. "You've come to the wrong address."

But the address was right enough when he checked it.

"Who sent you then?" her mum had demanded.

"A young lady rang up."

"Ruddy kids."

Marlene had done it. Must have been her. She'd flipped. In love with Stevie Manns and jealous of Ally's love for him. Knowing, if it ever came to it, and if Stevie had to choose between them, that she'd never have a chance.

And yet it was so absurd. She'd never even *seen* Stevie Manns, let alone *met* him. And she probably never would meet him either.

Dream on. Wherever Marlene Forrester was living, it certainly wasn't in the real world. She was definitely two sandwiches short of a picnic in her lunch basket. Where had she been standing when the brains were being handed out? At the back of the queue? Or had she been off sick that morning?

Stevie Manns and Marlene Forrester? Do me several hundred favours! She'd more chance of getting off with the Pope.

Still, at least it made some kind of sense now, and that in turn made it a whole lot easier to live with. Ally could even feel a certain sympathy for Marlene, a kind of pity almost. In love with Stevie. She could understand that. Who couldn't? Who wouldn't understand that you were bound to fall in love with the most beautiful and talented human being on the face of planet Earth?

No, that was fine.

Only Stevie was *hers* – Ally's. It was in the stars and Marlene, bless her, was born under the wrong sign. And besides, would Stevie Manns, who had the pick of the most beautiful women in the world with his wealth and fame and talent and daily gym workouts, would Stevie Manns really look at Marlene Forrester? Oh, Marlene, come down from the clouds.

Was Marlene so blinkered? So blinded by love? Could she really not see how ludicrous it was? Stevie Manns was *never* going to go out with somebody like Marlene Forrester, no matter how short and tight she wore her skirts, how high she put her hair up, or how much pocket money she spent in the Body Shop.

Poor Marlene. Poor, deluded Marlene. She just couldn't see it, could she? And so she took it out on Ally. She just couldn't see it. Pity was the only word. She was making such a terrible fool of herself.

She was riding for a fall.

6

THE FLY IN THE OINTMENT

Was there ever a parade without rain? A party without
a pooper? Nope. There's only one thing you can count
on in life and that is that you can't. Count on anything,
that is. Nothing ever quite goes as smoothly as you'd
like it to. There is always a fly in the ointment somewhere.

Not that Ally had much in the way of ointments – or
face creams or anything else for flies to get into in her
half-empty drawer of cosmetics. Most of the stuff in
there had been given to her by Cheryl and had gone
crusty or separated out. It no longer smelled like it was
supposed to, but had a faint whiff of vinegar.

Even when she saved up her pocket money for a bit of
a splurge on something new in the make-up line for
herself, Ally couldn't bank on being left alone to enjoy it.

"You're never wasting your money on that stuff, are
you?" her mum would say, when they were out shopping. "You're never putting *that* on your face?"

And when Ally had put it on her face and was all
ready to go out and show it to the world, further

discouragement came from her dad, in the form of, "Where do you think you're going then, in that lot?"

Well, nowhere special, actually Dad, if you want the truth. Where is there to go? Round to Pauline's more than likely, to listen to some Five Nine tracks. For a change, that's right. Yeah, I know, I know. You don't have to say it. Ha, ha, ha!

Yeah, Pauline's, probably. Or maybe the park. Or if it was a fine summer's night, they might hang about for while outside the Happy Shopper, getting spied upon by old ladies with leatherette shopping bags, who stared at you as if drinking a can of diet cola was the greatest crime ever committed.

As soon as there was a good moment, Ally told her mum about the tickets.

"Fifteen pounds?" Mum said. "That's a lot."

But Ally had expected that. It was almost a reflex action. If the tickets had only been fifteen pence she'd have said the same thing on principle.

"Fifteen pence? That's a lot, Ally!"

If they'd been giving them away for nothing, it wouldn't have been much different.

"Giving them away for nothing? That's a lot."

They could even have been paying you a fiver to take them away.

"Paying you a fiver to take them away? That's not much."

So "Fifteen pounds? That's a lot," it was then, and you went on from there.

Ally didn't say anything. It was best not to try to persuade her mum. She knew that it wasn't such a lot really. If she had said to her mum that she wanted an hour at the skating rink for her birthday, or maybe an hour at the Super Bowl, followed by pizzas for her and her friends, well, that would have been a lot more that fifteen pounds. A lot more than thirty too. (Because she was still hoping that her mum would pay for Pauline as well. Much as she wanted to see the Five Nine live, she didn't want to see them on her own. She wanted Pauline to be there – if only to catch Ally when she fainted. Always assuming, of course, that Pauline hadn't fainted first herself. Or maybe they'd fall together, and prop each other up.)

"Fifteen pounds, eh? That's a lot."

Ally bit her lip. Silence. A weapon in its own right.

Come on Mum, she thought, *have your moment of power and suspense and then give in and say yes. Don't let me down now. You know you've got a heart of gold really. You know you're a softie.*

"Well . . ."

Yup. Here we go. Grudging surrender. *So don't think you're getting it too easy my girl*, kind of thing. *Don't you go taking it for granted. It all costs money, you know.* And other popular refrains.

62

"Well . . . I guess so. And you'll want to take a friend, I suppose?"

She was red hot with those supposes, Mum was. Sometimes you'd look at her and swear she'd been young once herself.

"Can I then? Go to the concert?"

"All right. But only because it's your birthday." (*Reasons for Being Generous, part two.*) "And only because it's not on a school day. If it wasn't on a Saturday, you couldn't go. Of course, I'll have to check with your—"

You won't really though, will you Mum? Ally thought. *You say that, but he's just the rubber stamp, old Dad. It's all signed and sealed before he even gets home and rinses out his lunchbox.*

"I'm sure Dad won't mind, Mum."

And that was true. Dad would let her go to the moon, if it made her happy, and give her the pocket money for the trip.

Not that he was a soft touch. But he was pretty easygoing. There would be no dire consequences as far as he was concerned. In her dad's world, it was no bad thing to stand outside the Happy Shopper drinking diet cola. He didn't care.

"Not doing any harm, is it?" he'd say.

And as long as it did no harm, you could get on with it. So when he came home that evening and Mum said,

"Ally wants to go with a friend to see that pop group on her birthday. You know, the Five to Nine."

"*Five Nine*, Mum!" Honestly! Did she get it wrong deliberately?

"Yeah? What about it?" her dad said, as he dropped an apple core and clingfilm sandwich wrappers into the bin.

"Well, we want to know what you think," her mum said.

So what do you think, Dad? Go on, say the magic words.

"Well, why not. I can't see any objections. Won't be doing any harm, will it?"

He was a saint. Saint Dad. The man with the magic clichés.

"It's fifteen quid each," Mum told him, as if she expected him to say it was outrageous.

"Well, it's not every day you have a birthday," he said.

"You don't think we'll be spoiling her . . ."

Great, isn't it? Some people went away for four weeks holiday a year and skiing in the winter and got everything bought for them and a clothes allowance on top. Others ask for one treat and their mum gets worried that it might be spoiling them.

"No. Not at all. Why would it be spoiling her?"

Keep talking, Dad. You're saying all the right things here. Do you write your own material?

"So where is the concert?" he asked. "Wembley?"

"Er . . ." Ally hesitated. Now, there might be a slight problem here. Another little fly in that ointment, one she maybe hadn't mentioned.

"Well?" he said.

"Sort of Birmingham," she told them.

"Birmingham!" her mum exclaimed.

"Sort of."

"What do you mean *sort of* Birmingham? I mean, it *is* Birmingham or it *isn't*. What's *sort of* Birmingham?"

"Well, it *is* Birmingham then. It's at the NEC."

"The National Exhibition Centre," Dad said. "But that's in Birmingham."

"She just said it was in Birmingham," her mum told him with irritation.

"I know. But Birmingham, that's miles away," her dad said. "How are you going to get to Birmingham?"

"I thought we could go in the coach," Ally said.

"And how much is the coach?" her mum demanded, as if Ally was asking her to pay for it or something. Which she was. Or rather hadn't yet, but would be.

"And how are you going to get back?"

"Well, on the same coach, Dad."

"And what time will that be, when you get home?" her dad said, getting all parental and taking his responsibilities seriously. "The middle of the night, I suppose!"

65

"Yes. I don't know about this at all now," Mum said. "Two young girls getting on a coach on their own. Going up to Birmingham. And there'll be a big crowd, won't there?"

"Well, yes, Mum. It's a concert. That's what they have at concerts. Big crowds. If there were only the two of us going, there wouldn't be much point in them hiring the hall, would there?"

"Don't be cheeky to your mother, Ally," her dad said.

"I'm not! I'm just trying—"

"You could get lost in a big crowd," her mum was saying. (She'd gone into prophecy-of-doom mode.) "I was in a big crowd myself once and—"

Here we go, Ally thought. *Five minutes now on Big Crowds I Have Known and My Distressing Experiences With Big Crowds.*

"We'll be all right, Mum. Honest. I'll be with Pauline."

"You might get separated," her dad said.

"So we'll arrange to meet up."

"I don't know," her mum said. "I don't know at all."

Dad didn't know either. He was making the *I Don't Know Faces* and her mum was making the *I Don't Know Either Faces* to help him out.

It looked like her mum and dad were presenting the Solidarity Front. And when that happened, you knew you'd had it. There was no divide and rule with Ally's

66

parents You couldn't get a bus ticket between them. Why did they have to be so united over these things? Why couldn't they go through a bad patch and not get on for a while, and let their children manipulate them and play one of them off against the other, like normal people?

But no, no chance. Other people's parents had rows and got divorced. But not Ally's. Hers just stood shoulder to shoulder through thick and thin, and good times and bad, till death or football on the telly did them part.

Ally's heart dropped to her boots. She stood knee-deep in the dust of her shattered dreams.

"Isn't there a concert nearer?" her mum was saying. "They must be playing somewhere else."

"They're all sold out, Mum."

"You might get a cancellation," she said.

"You don't get cancellations, not at Five Nine concerts."

"Then how about going to see another group instead then?" her dad suggested.

See another group! Ally almost gasped out loud. He just didn't understand, did he? He simply did not understand. *See another group?* Was he mad? What other group was there to see? There was only one!

Mum was looking at Dad again, Dad was looking at

Mum. The real Solidarity Special now, the real, one hundred per cent genuine, cast iron, brick wall.

"What do you think?" he asked her.

"What do *you* think?"

Dad sucked in his breath. The way he used years ago, when he still smoked.

"Well . . . it's a long way to Birmingham. I don't know how late she'd be back."

"*Too* late. It's just far too late for girls her age to be out on their own."

"We'd get a taxi, Mum," Ally pleaded. "We'd get a taxi home from the bus station, honest. And we wouldn't talk to anyone. Promise."

"*If* you can get a taxi at that time of night, of course," her mum said doubtfully. "You wouldn't even be back at the bus station before one or two in the morning, would you?"

"Three or four, more like," Dad grunted

Thanks, Dad, thanks a bunch. Yeah. Make it a bit worse than it has to be.

"I've been at the bus depot at that time of night and sometimes there aren't any taxis at all," he continued. "So you take it into your head to start walking rather than wait, and then—"

"Exactly," her mum said. "Somebody follows you, a shadow in the darkness, or they offer you a lift, two young girls on their own . . ."

68

And that was it.

Ally could see that she had lost. They weren't going to let her go. She wasn't a weak character, quite the opposite, but to have got so near to seeing Stevie and now to have it all snatched away. She could have broken down and—

"But then again, mind . . ."

She was back in the running. Her dad was looking thoughtful, like a man finding his way round obstacles.

Don't stop there, Dad. Go on.

"Then again . . ."

Ally's spirits lifted.

"Then again there *might* be a way of doing it . . ."

Her spirits soared. They flew like eagles and then a bit higher still.

Go on, Dad, say the right thing. I'll come and visit you when you're old. And if you're good, you can have the spare room in the great big mansion where Stevie Manns and me will live happily ever after with our brood of five children. Or will it be six? (All right, Stevie, if you want six, and as you're such a good dad, six it is.) So be a good dad, Dad.

"Maybe the answer is—"

But just a moment, was that the cavalry coming to the rescue? Or was it more a bombshell that Ally heard falling?

"— that we *all* go! All of us! As a *family!*"

69

Oh my sweet sainted aunt nine times over. Go to see the Five Nine with your mum and dad! Sweet hole in the ground, swallow me up. Big one ton weight, please drop on my head. Nice, kind piranha fish, come swim around my bathtub. My mum and dad are going to come to the Five Nine concert with me. Please let me die.

Ally closed her eyes and was about to die, when she suddenly came back to life, revived by her mum's voice, saying:

"Go to a Five Past Nine concert? If you think I'm standing in the Birmingham NEC with a bunch of teenyboppers, sticking out like a vegetarian at the butcher's annual dinner, no thank you!"

"No, no, I didn't mean that," her dad said. "Not all go to the *concert*. I meant why don't we all go to *Birmingham*?"

"What for?"

"See the place."

"See Birmingham?"

"Yeah."

"Why?" her mum asked. "What do you want to see Birmingham for?"

"I've never been there," her dad said. "But Cadbury's have their chocolate factory up there, haven't they? You can get a tour and see the chocolate being made. And get a bit to taste too, probably."

"You already know what it tastes like. You eat enough of the stuff." Mum muttered.

He ignored her and went on, "And it's not that far from Stratford-on-Avon. We could go and have a look at that as well."

"What's in Stratford-on-Avon?" her mum said.

"You know, Shakespeare's birthplace."

"Oh, that," she said, without enthusiasm.

"We could see Anne Hathaway's cottage," her dad said, sounding surprisingly keen. "And have a ploughman's lunch after in one of the pubs."

"And where do we stay?" her mum demanded.

"In a hotel!" he announced, as if staying in hotels was an amazing, totally new concept that he'd just invented right then and there before their very eyes.

"Hotel?" Her mum almost shouted the word. "*Hotel!*"

It was as if someone had made an improper suggestion, like doing the housework in the nude.

"Hotels," she said gravely, "cost money!"

"That's all right," Dad said. "I saw a thing in the paper. A special deal. Besides, you're working, I'm working, I'm getting a bit of overtime now. You can't say we can't afford it. We haven't had a holiday in years, we never go anywhere. Let's a have a weekend away for Ally's birthday. Let's go and enjoy ourselves a bit. What do you say?"

Nothing for a second. She was gob-smacked speechless.

Poor Mum.

That was what years of being hard up did to you. Years of her being a little girl when gran and grandad were poor almost beyond imagining. It all seemed like extravagance to her now. Even small, inexpensive things that other people took for granted. Little treats, little trips.

It was always the thin end of the wedge for her mum, and she had to watch the pennies like a hawk, or the pounds might disappear. Yet what if you died and never enjoyed any of what you'd worked for? Wasn't that a waste too? You couldn't take it with you, after all. And even if you could, what would you spend it on when you got there? What did they sell in heaven? Harps and halos? What could you buy in hell? A fire extinguisher and an asbestos suit?

Ally's mum was obviously tempted though. Her mind was working overtime, seduced by thoughts of travel.

"Chocolate factory, eh?" she said. "Anne Hathaway's cottage? Shakespeare? Stratford-on-Avon? Staying in a hotel? Lunch in a pub?"

"A pub with a restaurant maybe," her dad said, sounding like he was due to start a new job soon as the last of the big spenders. "Needn't be a ploughman's. Not just bar snacks. Proper sit-down job."

You could tell he was getting carried away with himself.

"Well . . ."

Her mum did that thing with her hair then, like she always did when she was nervous or uncertain. And funnily enough, just for a moment, she looked younger than Ally.

"All right," she said. "All right! Then we'll go."

Ally could have hugged them. Both of them and everything in the room. Mum, Dad, chair, table, curtains, mugs, kitchen-roll holder, the lot.

Then *Zzzzzz!*

There it was: fly approaching ointment at five hundred miles an hour. When unstoppable fly collides with immovable ointment, what do you get?

Disappointed. That's what you get. Covered in a big sticky mess. And the fly's name in this instance was Cheryl.

"I've just thought! What about Cheryl?" her mum exclaimed, just when Ally thought it was all settled. "We can't leave her on her own."

"What's that about me?"

It was Cheryl herself. She had come in from her job at the hairdresser's. She was still only a trainee, but she had enough swank for a whole salon. She spent most of her day washing hair and saying, "Is that water too hot for you?" and "Would you like a cup of coffee?" and going round with the broom, sweeping all the hair up as the stylists cut it off. Then, if it was quiet, the senior stylist, Mr Rudolph (and that was never his real name) might let her stick a few rollers into a couple of wigs to try and get the hang of it.

But you'd think from the way she carried on that she was up for a leading role in Hollywood as Snipper To The Stars, and it was only a matter of how many million dollars they ought to pay her and how many rubies and diamonds she should have in the handle of her hair-brush.

"What about me? What were you saying?" Cheryl asked, as she took her coat off.

"We're thinking of going to Birmingham on Ally's birthday," Mum explained, "so she can see that Nine Forty Five group."

"*Fine Nine!*" Ally snapped. She was sure her mother was getting it wrong on purpose.

"Whoever. And we thought we might make a week-end of it, stay overnight somewhere—"

"In a *hotel*," Ally's dad said importantly. He seemed to like the sound of that word. You'd think that he'd invented it or something.

"– and have a look around."

Mum went to get the tea on. Cheryl looked blank.

"Well, you can count me out. I've already arranged something for the twenty-ninth. Sorry little sis."

"That's all right," Ally said. (And who was *she* calling little sis? She must have got that one off the telly, from one of the American sit coms or cartoons. *Little sis*

74

indeed.) "That's all right, Cheryl. That's all right, big sis," she replied.

Cheryl looked at her with heavily made-up but very narrowed eyes.

"Of course I'll be sorry to miss your birthday, Ally, and you must tell me what you want for a present. But I had arranged with—"

She hesitated. Ally knew, even if her mum and dad didn't, that what was coming next was going to be a lie.

"—arranged with Lyn to . . . go to a party that night."

"Oh, don't worry. Never mind," Mum said, "as long as you've something to do and won't be on your own."

It was go to a party with her boyfriend, more like, not with Lyn. And now she'd have the house to herself afterwards and all. And what would *they* be getting up to, Ally wondered? Well, hands up all those who've ever been to biology lessons. Yeah. Quite. Exactly.

"Well, it's a shame you can't come . . ." Dad was saying.

Speak for yourself.

"But if you've made other arrangements . . ."

"Will you be all right on your own, love?" Mum was twittering. "I know you're old enough but—"

"Yeah, don't worry about me," Cheryl said. "I'll be fine."

Well, yeah, Ally thought, *I mean, if a man got into the house or anything, you could always shout for your boyfriend, Mike, couldn't you? He's not likely to be too far away. One flex of his biceps and a flash of his well-brushed gnashers and they'd all be running off. I don't* think.

"Okay. Well remember to tell me what you want for your birthday, *little sis*."

"Okay, *big sis*."

And off big sis went to tart herself up in her bedroom. You'd think she'd have had her fill of mirrors for the day. The salon was full of them and you could see yourself from all angles, the back of your head and everything. You'd think it would get boring after a while, looking at yourself. But not for Cheryl. The back of her head interested her no end. And the front of her head, and her profile, and her figure, and how flat her stomach was that day. She couldn't see enough of herself, and most of her meagre wages went across one cosmetics counter or another, in endless pursuit of the perfect appearance.

"I don't know what you do with your money, Cheryl," Mum would say, about to go into *when I was your age* mode. But Ally could easily have told her where Cheryl's money went.

"She sticks it all on her face," Ally could have said, "and what's left goes on clothes. Most of them worn once and then put in the wardrobe, because she buys

76

them one size too small and they don't fit. And she buys them the wrong size in expectation of losing weight, because she's always going to go on a diet. But she never does; or she does, but it doesn't work; or it only lasts five minutes, and then she's back on the Hob Nobs."

But Cheryl might stop giving Ally her cast-offs then, if she actually did said that. So she wisely didn't say anything, and tried to smile nicely as Cheryl went up to her room.

"I can ring up the hotline then, can I Mum?" Ally said, anxious not to give her parents any time in which to change their minds. "And book the tickets? It's just I'll need a credit card number."

Mum looked a bit nervous at that.

"Hang on."

She went and got her credit card from its hiding place. She didn't carry it with her and she never used it.

"Why don't you keep it in your purse?" Dad had asked once.

"I might be tempted to buy something then," she said.

"That's the point of having it, isn't it? To buy things with?"

"I'm not getting into debt," she said, "for anybody."

She handed the card to Ally.

"Here. And be careful with it. And bring it straight back."

Like, don't lose it on your way to the sitting room, or get mugged as you walk past the airing cupboard. I mean, that was really likely to happen.

"When you've got the tickets, I'll ring up and book this hotel," Dad said. He showed them the newspaper where he had seen the special offer. "I'll get two rooms, eh? Adjoining ones. Mum and me in one, and you and Pauline next door." He looked at Ally. "Ally, hadn't you better check with Pauline and her parents first? About whether she can come?"

"Oh, yeah. I suppose I had."

She rang Pauline first. She was out, but she rang back within ten minutes and it was all okay.

"Great. Tremendous. We're on," Ally said. "Just need to think what to wear now. I'll get back to you on that." And she hung up.

Ally booked the tickets with her mum's credit card, and was told that hers and Pauline's names would also be automatically entered for the *Meet the Five Nine* draw. So even a backstage pass was possible – you never knew.

Then her dad got on the phone and he booked the hotel on the special deal weekend package, and he got two rooms for the price of one to also include breakfast. He said each room would have its own TV, air conditioning, *en suite* bathroom, mini-bar, kettle and trouser press. And loads of other things as well.

"All right," he said. "We're set."

"What time shall we aim to get there?" Mum said. "Late afternoon on the Saturday?"

That was fine by Ally. The concert didn't start until eight.

But "Oh no," her dad said. "No, no, we'll have to get there much earlier than that. I want to make a proper weekend of it. I want to get there by one o'clock on Saturday afternoon at the very latest."

"By one? Why one?" her mum said, a bit suspicious.

"Oh, didn't I tell you?" Dad answered. "Did I forget to mention it? City are playing away at Birmingham on the twenty-ninth. I thought that as we were going up there anyway, I may as well try and catch the game."

Mum's mouth dropped open like a window with the sash cords gone. All it lacked was the sound effects. The *kerwhoooomp* and the *bang-crash!*

"Of all the devious—" she began. But she caught Ally's eye then and saw her smile, and then the two of them were laughing. Dad smiled back, a bit sheepish, and he even blushed a bright red.

"I only thought," he stuttered, "you know . . . if we were going anyway . . ."

But they laughed at him until he had to laugh too. While upstairs, in her bedroom, Cheryl sat in front of the mirror, bringing her facial appearance one step closer to perfection as she grasped a wandering eyebrow with her stainless steel tweezers and gave it a sharp tug.

"Ooouch!"

She looked at the plucked hair, held between the two prongs.

You had to suffer in the cause of beauty.

7

MARLENE'S BODY BLOW

"A watched kettle never boils, Ally."

Thanks, Mum, she thought. *Thanks a bundle. Always helps, a drop of that old homespun wisdom. It'll be "A stitch in time saves nine next," and "Look before you leap".*

As if you'd never heard it before, Everyone's heard it before. But it makes no difference, people go on saying it anyway. But, really, why bother? Because everyone *knows* better, they just can't always *do* better. That's the thing. So what's the point in reminding them about what they know already, but can't control?

It's like going round saying war is a bad thing. Well everyone *knows* that. But how are you going to stop it? That's the point.

Ally was in the kitchen with a thick red pen in her hand, crossing off another day on the calendar.

"You're like one of those prisoners, in cartoons," her mum said, "who sit in a cell, marking the days off, until it's time to get out."

She was right there too. Ally was a prisoner, all right, a hostage to love, and there were just three weeks left now to freedom and escape. Escape from all this hum-drum, mum-drum, everyday routine.

Wake up, the routine went, go to school, come home, do your homework, go out at the weekends, hang round by the Happy Shopper or the Deep Sea Fry, try and avoid Marlene Forrester and stay out of her bad books. (Which wasn't so easy as Marlene had more bad books than a bad bookshop.)

And what was the future? Exams, leave school, a job, maybe, maybe not. Living at home until something happened to take her away from it all? Marriage, kids, who knows? It was like a relay race. One generation to the next. Carrying on as you were, until it was your turn to pick up the baton. And that *was* the baton round here: job, marriage, kids. Maybe, one way or another, that was the baton everywhere.

Or maybe there was a chance to be different. It had come some people's way. Jean Coles, for one. She'd gone off to be a model and had worked abroad, and her mum said that she was presently starring in a musical in a club in Turkey. Ally's mum had wrinkled her nose up at that, as if starring in a musical in a club in Turkey wasn't as much to be proud of as Jean Coles's mum made out.

Anyway, three weeks to go, and then a different kind of escape. Three weeks until she saw Stevie Manns in the flesh, up on the stage, singing *You Are My Heart* just for her.

*"You are my heart, my love, my life
One day soon you'll be my wife . . ."*

Fantastic. And somehow they'd meet after the concert. Quite how, Ally wasn't sure, she hadn't worked out the details. But maybe he'd spot her in the crowd. For a moment he'd forget the words of the song he was singing. He'd hold his hand up to shield his eyes from the dazzle of the stage lights. Then he'd recover, and finish the song. But before the next song started, he'd have crossed to one of the roadies at the side of the stage and said, "That girl, the one with the fantastic eyes, about halfway along in row twenty-five, find out who she is. I think . . . I've fallen in love."

Then Charlie would spot Pauline, and he'd fall in love with her too. (Because it wouldn't be very nice if Pauline got left out of everything and had to just sit about like a gooseberry.)

And it would just go on from there. Ally could already see it. The big heavy bouncer wending his way through the screaming crowd looking for her. Tapping her on the shoulder. Her surprise. Pauline's surprise. The shock, dismay and envy of everyone around them.

"Stevie and Charlie say they *have* to meet you," the bouncer would say. "Here's two backstage passes. Come round immediately after the show. And don't let them down, or they'll be broken-hearted."

Then the show goes on. But Ally and Pauline don't

seem to be there any more, because they're up on a cloud somewhere now – cloud number nine, probably – looking down on it all, like they've turned into angels.

And before you know it, the concert's over, and they're backstage, and actually *there* with Stevie and Charlie, and everyone's really up in the air and over the moon, it's been such a fantastic performance. And there's a party then, with everybody who's anybody going to it. And people are saying

"Who *is* that girl? *Is* she someone? Who *are* those girls? Are they *models?*"

But before anyone can answer that question, Stevie is by her side, and he's steering her away from the hubbub, and he's saying, "Ally, I need to talk to you. We have to be alone. Get Pauline and Charlie, and let's go to a quiet restaurant I know."

Because he would. You knew he would. He *would* know quiet restaurants. Expensive places with signs on the door saying *Ties Must Be Worn*. Only when they saw Stevie and Charlie coming they would take the sign down and the head waiter would greet them and say, "This way, sir. Don't worry about the tie rule. Naturally, it doesn't apply to you. Your usual table, is it, sir? Such a pleasure to have you back. And such beautiful young ladies with you tonight, sir. So obviously talented too. Not just lookers, but thinkers as well. This way ladies, if you would."

It would be candlelit dinners then and champagne; the popping of corks and the flickering of flames. And over the champagne and candlelight, Stevie would reach for her hand and say, "Ally, something strange and marvellous happened to me tonight. Something I never thought would happen. You see, I sing about love, we sing about love all the time. But what do I *really* know about love? What did I *ever* know about love? Until tonight. Ally, will you – I know it's sudden because we've only just met – but will you marry—"

"ALICE! ARE YOU UP THERE OR WHAT?"

It was flipping Cheryl, booming up the stairs like a foghorn on a dark night. And who asked her to butt in on people's fantasies?

"I'M GOING OUT. CAN YOU FEED THE CAT?"

Cat? Ally thought. *I ask you. Down to earth with a bump all right. One second Stevie Manns is about to ask you to marry him, the next you're feeding the cat.*

She hated Cheryl sometimes, she really did. The cat was half hers. Why couldn't she feed it once in a while?

Ally heard the door slam. She'd feed the cat in a minute. It was too fat anyway. Wouldn't do it any harm to lose a bit of weight. It never would though. That cat was the same as Cheryl. Always going on diets and never sticking to them.

Ally returned to her thoughts.

So how long was it now? Ah, still three weeks. How

slow the time goes when you want it to go fast. Maybe she'd go round and see Pauline. That might make the time go quicker.

She got up off the bed, went downstairs, fed the cat, petted her, combed her to get the bits out of her fur, and then called to her mum.

"Is it all right if I go and see Pauline, Mum?"

"I suppose, if you've done your homework."

"I have."

"All right. For an hour. But don't—"

"Be back late, I know."

And she was gone.

She found Pauline down outside the Happy Shopper. She was standing on her own. A crowd of boys was at the corner, drinking lager they were too young to have bought and smoking cigarettes that they'd only end up miserably addicted to, but which they thought made them grown up and cool.

Stevie Manns didn't smoke or drink. He was cool enough without it. Really cool people didn't need props. But the boys round her way smoked to look grown up. It didn't make them look grown up though. It just made them look like a bunch of kids *trying* to look grown up.

Still, that was their problem.

Clustered round a vandalised bench were some other girls, Marlene Forrester and Tracey Norris among them. Pauline looked a bit on her own, but she didn't seem to mind. She was eating a bag of chips – not so much out of hunger probably, but more to give herself something to do.

Ally went over and joined her.

"Hi, Ally."

"Hi, Pauline."

"Chip?" she offered.

"Ta." Ally took a couple.

"Listen, I was thinking," said Pauline.

"Thinking what?"

"Well, what are we going to wear?"

"What, on the big night?"

"Absolutely."

It was a question they had already discussed. But there was nothing wrong with discussing it again.

"Have you got anything, then?" Ally asked.

"I don't know. I mean, are you *supposed* to get dressed up?" Pauline said.

"Why, aren't *you* getting dressed up then?" Ally said.

"I don't know. I mean, how dressed up are you supposed to get?"

"Yeah, right. Take your point. I don't know."

"I thought I might wear my leather mini, actually," Pauline said. "What do you think?"

She'd bought the leather mini herself with her Saturday money. Much to her mum's disgust. And, of course her dad came out with the classic, the old favourite, the ever popular standby for such contingencies, "You're never going out wearing *that*, are you?"

So she'd been looking for a chance to wear it ever since.

Ally felt a bit jealous that she didn't have a leather mini. She'd never buy one though, not even if she *did* have the money, as she was big on animal rights and didn't wear leather. Because if meat was murder, what was leather then? It had to be manslaughter at the very least. And Stevie wouldn't wear leather. Nitz did of course. He was always in leather. Well, let's face it, he was probably made out of leather. But Stevie was a vegetarian too. Which only went to show that you didn't need to eat meat to have a few muscles and look fantastic.

"So what about you?" Pauline said. "What are you going in?"

Ally considered a moment.

"I'll wear *my* mini – the red one."

It wasn't leather, it was wool and cotton. But it was every bit as short as Pauline's, and had provoked very much the same kind of parental response.

"You're never going out in *that*, are you?" her dad had said. "You'll catch your death. If you are going out *in* it, of course. Because you look more out of it than in it to me. How did you get it on? With a shoehorn and pot of margarine?"

Her mum, though, had been unexpectedly suppor-
tive.

"Let her wear it. You're only young once."

"You'll only get frostbite on your bum" her dad had
said. "Then you'll never be able to sit down again. We'll
have to buy cushions for the toilet seats."

But he grudgingly gave way in the end.

"Well, if you want to go about looking like your
clothes shrank in the washing machine, I suppose it's up
to you." And he let her wear it to the school disco.

"The minis then?" Pauline said.

"All right." Ally took another chip. "The minis it is."

"How about tops?" Pauline said.

"Low," Ally reckoned.

"How about make-up?"

Ally wasn't sure.

"Stevie says he doesn't like a lot of make-up," she
said.

"*They* all wear make-up," Pauline protested. "In the
band."

"That's different," Ally said. "They're boys."

"Men."

"Men then. I mean, it's all right for men to wear make-
up. On stage, I mean. But Stevie says he likes things to be
more natural."

"Charlie likes make-up," Pauline reminded her.

"I never said he didn't," Ally said.

89

"I might wear some then."

"I might wear *some*," Ally said. "Just not too much. I'll just wear enough to look natural. I mean enough to make it look as though I haven't got any on."

Pauline looked at her, a chip in her hand.

"Excuse me, Ally. Did you hear what you just said?"

Ally took a chip from the bag without waiting to be asked. Share and share, that's how it was.

"Eh? What did I say?"

"You just said you were going to put on enough make-up to make it look as though you didn't have any make-up on."

"So?"

"Well if you want to look as though you haven't got any make-up on then the best thing to do is not to wear any."

"If I don't wear any," Ally said, "I'll just look washed out and pasty. Especially in the National Exhibition Centre in Birmingham. I mean, it's huge."

"Oh," said Pauline. "I see."

They each had another chip.

"What about hair?" Pauline asked. She went to run a hand through hers, but stopped herself when she saw the oil from the chips on her fingers.

"We'll get my sister to do it," Ally said. "She needs the practice, and she's always looking for people to experiment on."

"*Experiment* on!" Pauline said. "I don't like the sound of that. Who is she, Dr Frankenstein? I don't want her experimenting on *my* head."

"Looking for *models*, I mean," Ally said. "She's quite good really. Just needs the experience. She did Mrs Quinn's poodle, last week. Made a good job of it too."

"Poodle?" Pauline said. "Her *poodle?* I thought your Cheryl was doing hairdressing, not dog grooming."

"It's all pretty much the same thing," Ally said. "If you can do one, you can do the other. A lot of famous hairdressers started off doing dogs."

"Such as who?" Pauline said.

"Vidal Sassoon," Ally told her. "He used to do the Queen's corgis."

They had another two chips apiece.

"Are you sure about that?" Pauline said.

"Well, I think he did," Ally said. "At least, I thought I read it somewhere. There's a lot of salt on these chips, isn't there. I might nip into the shop and get a can."

She was looking for her money when a boy in baggy jeans, Nike trainers, and a sweatshirt approached. He was carrying a skateboard and wearing a baseball hat with NY on it. The hat was on back to front. He dropped the skateboard down on to the pavement and tested the springs with his foot.

It was Phil Roach from their class.

"Hello, Ally," he said. "Hello Pauline. You having some chips?"

"No," Pauline said, "I'm eating a pigeon. What does it look like?"

"There's plenty of them about," he admitted. "Pigeons. They're all over the place. Real nuisance, pigeons."

He didn't seem to know what to say next and just stood there, neither staying nor going, looking a bit like a tongue-tied lemon – if there is such a thing, and there might be, one day, with genetic engineering.

It was nerves probably. He didn't seem able to continue a conversation. At least not with girls. He was all right with his mates. And he was all right on the opening gambits, but the chat went downhill very rapidly after that. He tried to be all dynamic and cheerful to start with, but found he could never sustain it or live up to the promise of his opening banter, and it all generally petered out in about ten seconds flat.

But today he was making a special effort. Maybe he'd been practising. Maybe he'd memorised a list of things to talk about before he'd left home.

"So, how's it going?" he said.

"All right," Pauline drawled.

"Not so bad," Ally agreed.

They didn't bother asking how it was going for him.

"Your birthday soon, Ally, is that right?" he said.

"That's right."

"How did you know it was her birthday?" Pauline asked. "Was it on the news?"

"I remembered it."

Of course, he'd been to her birthday parties a few times. They'd been kids together, in and out of each other's houses years ago. But Phil's mum and dad had split up, and he'd been taken to live a few streets away, and that friendship had sort of petered out too.

It was thanks to Phil though that Ally knew she had fantastic eyes. He'd told her as much once, at the school disco. Mind you, they tell you anything at those discos. It's like the flattery game. They do it for a laugh half the time, and see if you're daft enough to fall for it. They tell you how beautiful you are just to see how much of it you'll swallow. Then you might hear them the next day laughing about it. A bunch of lads at the end of the playground, all chortling hilariously.

"Hey, you know that Tessa Brown?"

"What, her with the spots and the big bum?"

"Right. Well, I told her last night that she had hair like spun gold and the figure of a film star."

"Which film star was that? Lassie the dog?"

"Nellie the elephant?"

"King Kong's big sister?"

"No, that actress in that film on at the Multiplex. But the thing was that she *believed me!*"

And it brought the house down.

And they said that girls could be cruel and bitchy, that boys used their fists and girls used their tongues. But it wasn't true. Not in Ally's experience. There was pleasant, and there was unpleasant, and you got it everywhere.

But Phil wasn't like that. He was all right. Not her type or anything. More Pauline's type than anyone's, if you were going typecasting. It was Ally he was after though, and she wasn't interested. She had Stevie Manns. How could Spots on a Skateboard compare to Stevie?

Not that Phil was *that* spotty. Well, he wasn't actually spotty at all. Maybe he had been once, and someone had said, "Here comes Spots on a Skateboard," and it had stayed with him ever since.

But Phil was all right. He had asked Ally to dance during one of the slow numbers at the disco. There they all were, dancing close, with Mrs Nary going about making sure no one got *too* close. In fact she used to bring a torch with her to school discos and she'd flash it at you and shout: "Wandering hands, wandering hands!" and even blow her netball whistle if she had to, to get the wandering hands to stop wandering.

You wonder she didn't go about handing out yellow cards and awarding penalties, and giving free kicks for being off-side on the dance floor, or start sending people off for scoring after the whistle had gone.

Anyway, Phil hadn't got *too* close – just close enough, and he had looked at her and said, "You know, Ally, I think you've got really fantastic eyes."

And that was it. Nothing else. Just fantastic eyes.

"Thanks," she had muttered.

She couldn't think of what else to say.

"Give us a chip then," Phil said.

Pauline screwed the wrapper up.

"Too late. All gone."

"Ah."

He was stuck for conversation once more. He brightened up and thought of something.

"It's your birthday soon, isn't it, Ally?" then he blushed. "Oh, yeah, I just said that, didn't I."

"Yes," said Pauline. "You did."

There was yet another uncomfortable pause.

"So what're you doing for your birthday then?" Phil managed to ask. "Skating rink?"

Ally exchanged a look with Pauline.

"We're going to see the Five Nine as a matter of fact," she announced.

Bombshell time. Her words echoed around the precinct. The cluster of people at the nearby bench fell silent and looked in her direction. She could feel Marlene Forrester's eyes prickling death rays into the back of her neck.

"Oh," Phil said, trying to keep the conversation

going. "You're big Five Nine fans then, are you?"

"None bigger," Pauline said. "Truly enormous."

Ally half-turned. She saw from the corner of her eye that Marlene Forrester and Tracey Norris had split from the group and were making their way towards them. She hoped there wasn't going to be trouble.

"I'm more of a blues fan myself," Phil was saying. "You know, the old stuff." Pauline looked at him as though she were glazed over with double glazing plus thermal curtains. "And I quite like some folk music. Folk rock and that."

Pauline shut the curtains and drew the blinds at that.

Phil could tell he was getting nowhere. You didn't need a GCSE in Getting Nowhere to see that. Folk and blues were plainly very much a minority interest round at the Happy Shopper. He returned to topics of more immediate interest.

"So who's your favourite in the Five Nine then?" he asked. (He was quite getting the hang of keeping the chat flowing now. He'd definitely oiled his squeaks.)

"Stevie!" Ally said immediately.

"Charlie!" Pauline said. "Who's yours?"

"Me? I haven't got one," Phil said. "I mean, it's a girls' band."

"What does that mean?" Pauline said, getting prickly. "Girls' band?"

"You know, girls scream at them."

"Girls screamed at the Beatles. Didn't stop my dad liking John Lennon," Ally said.

"I bet he didn't scream at him though," Phil continued. "He probably just wanted to *be* him. See, there's girls' bands and there's boys' bands, and then there's bands that everyone likes. But the Five Nine, they're a girls' band, aren't they? It's girls who buy the records."

"Doesn't mean boys don't like the Five Nine," Ally said defensively.

"No," Phil agreed. "But boys like bands like the Five Nine just because girls scream at them. And then they can imagine that if they were in them, everyone would scream at them too."

"Why, is that what *you* imagine?" Pauline said. "People screaming at you?"

"To be honest," said Phil, "sometimes, yes."

"Then you must be a weirdo," Pauline said.

"I bet I'm not," Phil told her. "I bet if you did a survey . . ."

Neither Pauline nor Ally volunteered to go round with the questionnaire, but Ally looked at him with a sort of . . . well . . . interest that she had never felt before. There might be some truth in what he was saying. There was a bit more to him than she'd thought.

"So when are you seeing them, the Five Nine?"

"On my birthday," Ally said. "I said, didn't I?"

"Ah, right."

Marlene Forrester and Tracey Norris had stopped right beside them now. They were just standing there eavesdropping on the conversation and making no pretence about it either.

"So where are you seeing them?" Phil said. "Wembley?"

"No, Birmingham. NEC." Ally said.

"That's miles, isn't it?"

"We're stopping overnight," she told him.

"So are *we!*" another voice said. And it was Marlene's.

They couldn't ignore them any longer. You could ignore them for a while. But once they started to actually intrude upon your conversation, you had to put up or shut up or shut *them* up, one of the three.

"I beg your pardon?" Pauline said. "Did you speak? Aren't you supposed to put your hand up first?"

"Why, is this a private conversation then?" Marlene smirked, and Tracey Norris did her loyal-follower bit and smirked too, to show solidarity. "You were talking so loud I thought it must be a public one.

"No," Pauline said. "It is a private conversation. Though if you're bored and looking for something to do, you can always push off. I'm sure the exercise would be good for you."

"Well, if you don't want other people to hear what you're saying, maybe you should keep your voice down," Tracey Norris chipped in.

"Maybe *you* shouldn't have such big ears," Ally said.

"Are you trying to be funny, Ally Morgan?" Tracey demanded.

"Why do you ask?" Ally came back. "Are you trying to be intelligent?"

All the while Phil Roach was just standing there not quite knowing what to do. He looked like a solitary policeman, trying to prevent a major riot all on his own, wishing that either reinforcements would turn up or that he could disappear before the trouble started.

"Is everything all right –" he began vaguely.

"Why don't you go and talk to your mates, Phil Roach," Marlene Forrester suggested.

"Yeah, go and play with your skateboard," Tracey said. "Do a wheelie on it."

"He'll do a wheelie on you, if you're not careful," Pauline said.

"Oh, would you, Phil? Would you do a wheelie on me?" Tracey said.

"Be a good idea if somebody did," Pauline said.

Phil looked at Ally. What did *she* want him to do? To go, or to stay?

"Go on, Phil. It's all right."

"You be all right, Ally?"

"Of course I'll be all right. Why shouldn't I be?" She looked dismissively at Marlene and Tracey. "Nothing to worry about here."

Phil hesitated. Hesitation was in his nature. He'd hesitate before dying. It made Ally want to shake him sometimes, shake some spontaneity into him.

"I'll be over with the lads then," he said, and then added a bit wistfully, "if anybody wants me." As if he felt nobody ever would.

He's so awkward sometimes, Ally thought, as she watched him go over to join his friends. *He's not bad looking, but he hasn't got much confidence. Maybe it's because he's from a broken home? A result of his parents splitting up?* You read about things like that in the Agony Columns. Cheryl never read anything else.

But then she remembered that she herself often felt insecure and inferior and unwanted. And she didn't come from a broken home. So where did that leave you? Except back at square one. It was down the snakes every time. As soon as you got to the top of a ladder, there was a great slippery python, just waiting for you.

"So who's *he* then? Your Knight in Shining Armour?" Marlene was saying, as Phil walked away out of ear shot. "Loyal protector or something, is he?"

"Why? Who are you two?" Pauline answered. "Beavis and Butt Head? Or is it more Wallace and Gromit?"

"Was there something you wanted, Marlene?" Ally said. "Something you had to say? Because if there wasn't—"

"Oh, we just couldn't help but hear what *you* were saying –" Marlene answered smugly.

"About the Five Nine concert at the NEC." Tracey chimed in.

"Oh yeah?"

"We're going as well. We've got tickets too."

"Oh, have you?" Pauline said drily. "That's nice."

"So what night are you going?" Ally said.

She didn't really need to ask the question. There was only one night they *could* be going. The same night as them. It was a series of three concerts, on the Friday, Saturday and Sunday nights. But there was no way it could be the Sunday, as Marlene would never get back in time for school on Monday morning, and there was no way Marlene's father would let her take a day off. And there was no way it could be the Friday either, because that would have meant missing the afternoon at school in order to drive up in time to get there.

So it had to be the Saturday. The same night as Ally and Pauline were going. The twenty-ninth. It had to be.

"What night are *you* going?" Marlene countered.

"The twenty-ninth, if it's any of *your* business," Pauline said. "Why?"

"Oh, what a coincidence! The twenty-ninth! That's when *we're* going. Aren't we Trace?"

Tracey, the Abominable Yes Woman, nodded her head.

101

"Yes! You know, I do believe we are!" she said. "Or maybe I should check the tickets."

"What row are you in?" Marlene said.

"What row are *you* in?" Ally answered.

"Forty-eight."

Thank heaven for that.

"*We're* in twenty-five!" Pauline gloated. "We're nearer the front than you."

So stick that on the end of your chopsticks! Drop that in your wok and stir fry it!

"Twenty-five?" Tracey said. "I wouldn't want to be that near the front. You don't get the wider picture."

"Well, I think forty-eight's too far back. You won't see anything there."

"There's bound to be a big video screen."

"Not the same as in the flesh."

So, Ally and Pauline had won the battle of *Who's Got The Best Seats*. What was coming up next? What would they do now to get one up? Hold a *Who's Got The Shortest Mini* contest? Or maybe Marlene Forrester was going to get her nose pierced for the occasion and stick a stud in it, and have *I Love Stevie* tattooed on her head or . . .

If only Ally had known in advance. If only she'd had some warning, some inkling, some suspicions, some sign. How could her usually so reliable sixth sense have let her down?

It was the way of the world. The way it always went. She got one over on Marlene, Marlene got one over on her. It was a petty, small-minded, silly childish game. But that's all it was usually: petty and small-minded and no one really got hurt.

So a body blow like this came all the harder for coming so unexpectedly.

The smirk should have told her that Marlene had serious ammunition. That superior smile was a storm warning in itself. Marlene stood there grinning like a bad news bear. A bad news bear with its claws at the ready and a defenceless dinner in its sights.

"So what'll you two be doing after?" Marlene said, almost chattily.

"After what?" Ally asked.

"And who wants to know anyway?" Pauline said, with a bit more aggression. But Marlene didn't snap back at her. She just went on talking in a calm, almost evil, voice. And that smirk never left her face.

"I mean after the concert?" she said.

"We haven't planned yet," Ally hedged.

"But we can tell you one thing," Pauline said, and she did a bit of smirking herself, "we won't be coming straight home. We're staying in Birmingham. In a hotel. With a trouser press!"

"We're staying over too," Tracey said.

"Hotel?" Pauline asked.

"No, with my cousin," Marlene admitted.

So Ally and Pauline had won the battle of the accommodation as well. And yet still Marlene and Tracey, the Abominable Smirk Face, went on grinning away like two vampires who'd accidentally got locked in at the blood bank overnight.

"So you'll be going back to your hotel after the gig then?" Tracey the Human Smirk said.

"Might be. Why?" Pauline asked.

"Never guess where *we'll* be going after?"

"Kentucky Fried Chicken, for a bucket of drumsticks each?" Pauline suggested. But Marlene still didn't rise to the bait.

Then she finally came out with it It was only one word. But it might as well have been a nuclear bomb.

"Backstage."

Ally reeled. Her head span. Her heart thumped. She clutched at the lamppost for support.

"What? What did you say?"

"Backstage. Me and Tracey are going backstage. You know that if you're in the Five Nine fan club, when you buy your ticket over the phone they put your name into this draw? And the winners get to go backstage that night and meet the group and everything? Well, my number came up. So two backstage passes. For me and Trace. Great, eh? Aren't you pleased for us? What a piece of luck, eh, don't you think? I thought you'd like to know. I was sure you'd want us to tell you. Just imagine, me and Trace, we'll actually get to meet Stevie and Charlie, and Nitz and Bobby R. Just imagine. *And* we get to go to the party after as well. Fantastic eh? Don't you think?"

But Ally couldn't think, not clearly, not of anything. She felt physically sick. She didn't know if it was rage or jealousy or disappointment or a sense of injustice. *Marlene Forrester*! Of all the people who should never, never, *never* have won that backstage pass. Of all the most undeserving people. How could she? How could they? How could there be any fairness, any justice? How could Mrs Nary say there was a God in heaven. How could she? When He let things like this happen? When He ignored the good and the righteous, and He let Marlene Forrester and Tracey Norris get the backstage passes for the Five Nine concert?

She wouldn't cry though. Later, maybe, but not now. Not in front of those two simpering faces. Those eyes, hungry for a sight of the hurt inside her.

Well, think on and look on. That was one thing they wouldn't see, no matter how long they stood and gawped. Not in a month, or even a whole year, of Sundays. And somehow Ally managed to shape her mouth into the semblance of a smile and say, "Hey, that's great. Tremendous. You're really lucky. You must be over the moon."

Over the moon and the stars and light years into space. That kind of happiness came once every thousand years.

But yes, she was actually able to *congratulate* them.

"Yeah, great, eh?" Marlene said. "Thought you'd be pleased for us. We'll tell you all about it when we get back. And that's a promise."

"Yeah. Be sure to do that," Ally said. She nudged Pauline with her elbow.

"Yeah," Pauline said. "You must."

"See you then," Marlene said.

"See you," echoed the Abominable Yes Woman.

And Marlene and Tracey were gone.

Ally and Pauline stood in silence, petrified, turned to stone.

"Hey, what's up?" a voice said. "Everything all right?"

It was Phil, coming back on his skateboard. Ally and Pauline shot him a look that said it all.

Not now, Phil. Not now, if you wouldn't mind. Bad time.

He took the hint and rolled on his way to practise jumps on the Happy Shopper unloading ramp. Someone came out after a minute or two and told him to stop the clatter.

Ally looked at Pauline. She saw the same outrage, hurt and anger that she felt herself, expressed in Pauline's face. Pauline's eyes brimmed with tears of disappointment. She thumped the lamppost with the side of her hand.

"Them!" she said. "Them! They gave the backstage passes to *them!*" And then the anger gave way to the pain and the tears cascaded from her eyes. "Oh, Ally," she cried. "Ally, they're going to see Charlie! They're going to see *Charlie*."

"I know, Pauly, I know. Don't cry. Please don't cry."

Pauline sat down on the bench and wept.

"What's up, Pauline?" someone shouted.

"What's up, with Pauline, Ally?" people called.

"She's all right. Leave her be."

Ally sat next to her to try and comfort her, but her own tears began to fall. She leant forward so that her hair shielded her face. She wept quietly, so that no one would hear her and no one would know. Especially not Marlene. If she looked back at them now, all she would see would be Ally sitting on the bench, and Pauline next to her. They might be killing themselves with laughter for all she knew.

"Oh, Ally," Pauline wept, "I feel so sad. It should have been me. I was so happy just to be going to the concert. But now I'm not any more. Not when I know that they're going to see them. Actually *see* them. Stand right next to them. Oh, Ally, it should have been me."

Should have been me, you mean, thought Ally. It was *her* birthday after all, not Pauline's. It was her dad paying for the hotel and her mum paying for the tickets. But she didn't say anything. She understood, only too well.

After a while their tears stopped and they walked home together. They parted company by Pauline's front gate.

"You all right now, Pauly?"

"I'm okay. Are you okay?"

"I'm okay. Don't let your mum see you've been crying."

"No."

"See you tomorrow."

"See you."

And Pauline went on up the path.

When Ally got in, she headed straight up for a bath.

"You all right, Ally?" her mum called from the living room, as she heard the back door open. She had to yell over the sound of the television. Ally swallowed hard and took a minute to reply.

"I'm fine, Mum. Just fine," she called back, trying to sound normal.

The television went off. Her mum was at the foot of the stairs now, looking up at her on the landing.

"You sure you're all right?"

"Positive."

"You don't sound it. You sound blocked up. Are you getting a cold?"

"No. I'm fine. Maybe a bit of one. But I'm fine. I'll have some hot lemon later."

As she had her bath, she listened to the radio. The DJ played a Five Nine track.

"A beautiful ballad. One for all you lovers," he said.

It was *Tears Cry No More*. And Ally sang – and cried – along with it.

"*Tears cry no more*," Stevie sang,

"*No more can I say,*
I loved you so much
But you went away

Now I'm alone
Alone at your door
Answer my prayer
Tears cry no more."

She felt a little bit better. She saw the last of the tears drop from the end of her nose and fall into the bath water. She wiped her face with the sponge. The tears were gone. Droplets in the ocean.

She felt so sad. So sad and so hurt. Was this what love was like? Was it *always* like this? And if so, then why did people sing about it and say how glorious it was, when it was all so painful and it hurt you so much?

All the time, every day, all the pain of hearing his voice and seeing his picture, of knowing that it never could be, but not for a moment ever doubting that it *would* be. Must be. Had to be. Knowing that it was hopeless, but never giving up hope. Because otherwise, she couldn't go on. She would simply cease to be. Just be extinguished, like a light in a room at the flick of a switch. She would turn to darkness.

She felt so sad and so aching that she could have drowned herself in that bath. But there was one thing that stopped her. One other emotion which came to outweigh all the rest.

Anger! Pure outrage at the sheer injustice of it! If there was any way of putting things right, she'd find it. And as for Marlene Forrester, she hated her more than she'd hated anyone in her whole life. It was perfectly clear to Ally now. Marlene Forrester was worse than Adolf Hitler.

8

TRANSFORMATIONS

The hours and the minutes, as Ally counted them, passed by like snails with rheumatism. But second by second they did go by, until finally the weeks turned to days, and then the days headed for the big day itself.

The tour was going well. Terrific reviews, great notices. A bit snooty, of course, in some of the music magazines, but then they always were.

Five Nine Mania Sweeps UK, read the headline on her father's paper. But of course that had probably been written by some middle-aged fat bloke who was losing his hair.

What did *they* know? What *could* they know? They didn't and couldn't, and so they used words like *mania* to make it seem trivial, just like it was some kind of summer madness that would be gone as soon as the cooler weather came.

They just didn't understand. This wasn't only for *now*, this was *forever*, this was for *life*. There was no going back on this, no growing old. This wasn't a fad or some passing craze. It was for always and ever more.

So the weeks turned to days, and not even Ally's jealously of Marlene Forrester (and it *was* jealousy) could completely mar the pleasure she felt in looking forward to the big night.

"It was a slow drip, drip, drip of mounting tension –" Ally read.

She was sitting in class *getting on with something* while Mrs Nary finished some marking. Even from where Ally sat, you could smell the stale tobacco smoke on Mrs Nary's clothes. She was a hardened smoker, though she never lit up where any pupils might see her, as she didn't want to set a bad example. But sometimes Ally would spot her in town, shuffling along with a cigarette in her mouth, almost as if she were following it down the road, like the Pied Piper. Unable to give up herself, she was always warning others against it.

"Whatever you do, *never* – I repeat – *never* start smoking. You'll only ever regret it. Far more than you can ever imagine."

Well, as far as Ally was concerned, she was willing to take Mrs Nary's word for it. To get so addicted that you couldn't even last a day without a cigarette, well, it wasn't Ally's idea of being your own person. You were no better than a slave. A slave to the tobacco companies. Who made a right mug out of you really, getting you addicted to the stuff, making out it was all cool and everything, and then once you were hooked and you couldn't give up, you gave them half your wages as you couldn't stop. No thank you. And poor old Mrs Nary had a terrible hacking cough as well.

"Now listen – (*cough*) – you lot – (*cough, cough, phlegm*) – whatever you do – (*cough, snort*) – never be beguiled – (*cough*) – into taking up – (*coughetty, coughetty, cough*) – smoking." (*Cough, cough, double phlegm, hack, wheeze, out with the hanky, spit, eeech, and on with the lesson.*)

It was enough to put you off your lunch. If it got any worse she'd be bringing in oxygen with her. Wheeling in a big cylinder and parking it by the desk.

No joke either. Ally's grandad had died of that: emphysema, a disease of the lungs, where the tissue wastes away and you can't breathe any more. Horrible. Slow suffocation. And that was all thanks to smoking. (Not that the Marlboro Man would bother to mention *that* to you if he didn't have to.)

So the time crept on, and the tension mounted with it. That *drip, drip, drip of mounting tension* just like in the crime book she was reading, about this woman detective.

It was all right for a bit of read, the book. It was called *Rampage Remembered*, and this woman detective in it was all hard-boiled and on the case and walking down the mean streets and all that sort of stuff.

But it was a bit phoney too. At least Ally thought so. It

was as if someone had said, "Why should private detectives always be men? I know, we'll have a woman one, that'll redress the balance and provide positive role-models for impressionable girls."

And maybe that was all well and good too. But somehow in this instance, it didn't sit right. Because the heroine wasn't *really* a woman detective at all, she was a woman playing at being a man detective, basically a man in a skirt (when she wore one, which wasn't often, her being so hard-boiled and everything). Whereas, surely, real women detectives would do things differently and in their own way, and not be imitation men but individuals in their own right. And they wouldn't go round solving everything with a punch on the nose and a sock on the jaw, they'd be a bit cleverer than that. And afraid sometimes too. But this woman was *never* afraid. And Ally didn't believe that for a moment.

So she sat in the class reading, as the drip, drip, drip of mounting tension dripped away like a leaky shower head, and while Mrs Nary did her marking, probably dreaming of her next fag.

Five days to go now, Ally thought, a mere five days. One hundred-and-twenty hours from now and they'd be on their way. How would she stay the pace and go the distance? A butterfly farm had already taken up residence in her stomach, and whatever food she ate just seemed to go straight though her.

114

"You're losing weight," her mum had said a few days ago. "You'd better not start getting anorexic, my girl, or I'll hold you down and force feed you chips and Mars Bars till you're back up to speed."

Ally's mother was a big embarrassment sometimes. When other mothers thought their daughters had eating problems, it was all tiptoing round on eggshells and quiet chats in corners, and soft words in delicate ears, and being sure not to upset anyone's tender feelings for fear of making things worse.

Not with Mrs Morgan. It was up front and out in the open with her. She'd done it with Cheryl as well, and Ally could remember her mum standing outside the bathroom door, the time she was afraid that Cheryl had got bulimia, rattling the door knob and saying, "Cheryl, what are you doing in there? You're not wasting all that nice dinner I made for you?"

"No, Mum," Cheryl said. "I'm just brushing my teeth."

"Good. Because I was half an hour cooking that."

Throw up your dinner! You wouldn't dare. Chance and privacy would be a fine thing round their house.

Her mum had gone and hidden the scales after that incident.

"I know what you two are doing. You're going in there weighing yourselves ten times a day. So from now on the scales are kept under lock and key and they come

115

out once a week. We're not having a whole load of eating disorders in *this* house!"

"Quite right," Dad said. "We're not having it."

Mind you, his eating disorder was that he couldn't get a big enough potato to stick into his mouth all at once.

"I've got worms," he used to tell everyone. "I've got to feed them to keep them happy."

And when Ally had been small, she'd actually believed him, and she'd followed him round the house going:

"Can I see your worms, Dad? Can I? Please?"

And he'd said no, as they were special hush-hush worms, doing secret work for the government, and he wasn't allowed to show them to anyone – not even his nearest and dearest – as it could mean the death of several British agents presently working under cover on enemy territory.

And she'd even believed that too.

What a load of garbage!

It made you wonder why you used to be so stupid.

Five days, and the *drip, drip, drip of mounting tension* went on dripping and mounting. If this was how you felt when you were just going to be in the audience, how did it feel to be actually up there on the stage? To be looking down on all those screaming, shouting, crying, happy, tearful, hysterical faces. To feel that maybe your throat would lock up and not a note would come out. That you suddenly couldn't remember the guitar chords to *Bad Times Are Like A Stranger*. That you couldn't remember the dance routine for *Better By Far My Heart*. The dreadful panic of stage fright, the terror of disappointing everyone.

Ally felt nervous enough and all she had was audience fright, but stage fright, that must be a million times worse.

She and Pauline had got the clothes for the evening all sorted out. In fact the clothes were so sorted out that Pauline had packed hers. She'd had them packed for two weeks now, "So as I won't have to rush on the day."

The make-up was more or less decided on too. They'd put quite a bit of work into that, and had experimented with several styles and looks. They'd even gone and sought advice from the woman at the cosmetics island in Lewinson's, the big department store.

They'd worried that she was going to be a bit snooty to start with, and she certainly looked it. She must have had about three cans of hair-spray on her bouffant and the foundation (or whatever she had on her face) was that thick you could have measured it with a dipstick. Her lipstick looked like Crown Gloss as well and she was wearing this white sort of overall thing which made her look half-medical and half like some kind of up-market toilet attendant.

Anyway, they'd plucked up their courage and gone

over to the counter and asked her advice. And quite honestly, pie couldn't have been nicer. She was *really* friendly. And *really* helpful. Explained all about different looks and how to go about them, and she gave them a dab of all the samples and a sniff of all the testers, and she was really, really nice.

True, she did try and flog them about two hundred quid's worth of cosmetics, ("Must have thought we were rich kids, Ally, eh?" "It's our style, Pauline, natural *style*") but she was only doing her job. And they thanked her kindly and said they'd be thinking about it and would probably be back ("Yeah, just as soon as we've held up a building society," Pauline said later) and they went on their way.

Her advice wasn't good enough for Pauline though.

"I want a second opinion," she said. And she hauled Ally into Meersham's, the second biggest department store in town, and dragged her round a few of the cosmetic islands in there too.

"When I leave school," Pauline said, "maybe that's what I'll do. Be a beauty consultant. Have my own cosmetics island in one of the big stores."

Ally made all the right noises at that, but when she looked around, she didn't much fancy it. It must be hard work, all that smiling and being nice to people, especially when you weren't in the mood. And what time did you have to get up, for heaven's sake? You must have to get up at about five in the morning to get all your *own* make-up on. Because all those assistants, they all looked like they were off somewhere. To a wedding, or a nightclub, or a TV studio. But they weren't though. They were just off to Meersham's on the bus, to stand about for the next eight hours on a pair of toe-crushing stilettoes, giving themselves back problems and varicose veins.

Didn't seem like fun and glamour to Ally. Seemed more like torture.

Anyway, the way it turned out, the second opinions weren't much help. Everyone recommended something different – like what *they* were selling on *their* counter, and nothing else would do. (*Surprise, surprise!*)

"I wonder," said Ally, "if all these creams aren't a bit of a con. Forty pounds for a little jar of skin revitaliser. How can it be worth that?"

A grey-haired, posh-looking woman in a red suit – who was in the middle of buying the stuff – overheard Ally:

"My dear, you don't *need* skin revitaliser. You have youth. And that's worth a good deal more than forty pounds a jar. But for those of us who ran out of youth some time ago, skin revitaliser at forty pounds a bottle is the best we can hope for. And cheap at the price too."

She gave them a smile then, a smile which looked like a very expensive one, with a lot of dental work, face-lifts, collagen implants and cosmetic surgery involved in its construction. Neither Ally nor Pauline had been able to think of anything to say to the woman – not at such short notice, though given a bit of time, they probably could have done. They simpered like a couple of idiots and went out by the nearest door.

They ended up with a jar of something from the Body Shop in the end, and said they'd share that. They already had the other stuff: mascara, eyeliner and all that. And what Ally didn't have she could always borrow from Cheryl. Or pinch from Cheryl, if it came to it. Well, borrow without asking on a non-returnable basis.

Cheryl was being pretty good about it all though, and actually coming up trumps for once – which didn't happen often with a badly shuffled pack of cards like her. But this time she was sweet as honey. She not only offered to do Ally's hair, she said she'd do Pauline's as well. And no charge.

"She just wants to experiment on us," Ally said suspiciously. "Maybe you were right, Pauline. By the time she's finished with our heads, we'll look like something out of a vivisection laboratory."

"Don't be so mean," Pauline said. "She *is* your sister."

"Exactly," Ally said. "And you don't know her like I do. You don't know what she does in the bath-room."

"I think you should give her the benefit of the doubt."

"Sometimes I think I should give her the benefit of a dose of rat poison in her tea."

"You don't mean that."

"I will do, if she messes my hair up."

But she hadn't. She'd done a great job. Absolutely fantastic. You could see she was a natural and that she'd chosen the right career. She wouldn't be staying at Head Bangers with Mr Rudolph for much longer (and Ally had finally found out that Mr Rudolph's real name was Derek). She'd be moving on to Nicky Clarke's or somewhere and becoming a top stylist. Or maybe even opening her own salon one day. She'd have to change her name, of course. She couldn't call it Cheryl's any more than Derek could call himself Derek. She'd have to call it something more exotic. Chez Cheryeel maybe, a bit French. Or something zany, like Short Back And Sides, or Back and Short Sides, or Short Sides Is Back. Or use a made-up name, like Yechrfl's, which nobody could pronounce and which sounded like a Polish vodka. And she'd have to make people wait two months at least for an appointment, so they'd all know how busy she was, even if she wasn't. That sort of thing was good for business.

She did their hair on the Friday night. It was a bit of a risk, really, as they were off on the Saturday, and if anything had gone wrong, there was no time to grow a bit back on or anything. But it was really great. She cut Pauline's into a kind of urchin cut, which make her look a good two years older at the very least – though you'd have thought the opposite would have happened and an urchin cut would have made her look younger. She left Ally's hair more or less the length it was at the back, but cut it differently at the front and the sides. It sounded like another of Cheryl's famous recipes for absolute disaster, but it turned out great as well.

"Thanks, Cheryl," Ally said.

"That's all right. And both have a good time tomorrow."

Ally thought she knew why Cheryl was being so friendly. It was because they were all going away for the weekend, and she we going to have the house to herself. Herself and her boyfriend Bruce that is.

His name wasn't *really* Bruce, of course, it was Michael. But Ally called him Bruce because he was a dead ringer for Bruce Willis in a vest – minus his charisma and star quality. He had the muscles though and he was always dead keen to get his shirt off at the first ray of sun. The other main difference was that Bruce Willis probably bought his vests in Beverley Hills, whereas Mike got his from Primark.

"What do you think of him?" Cheryl had asked, the first time she'd brought him home.

"He looks like Bruce Willis," Ally said. "Only Bruce Willis's vests are cleaner."

"His vest was *dirty*," Cheryl said, "because he was working on his car."

"Is he a mechanic then?" Ally asked.

Cheryl went into haughty mode then, like there was something wrong with being a mechanic. Which Ally thought was pretty rich. Their own dad was a sort of mechanic after all.

"Michael," she said, (and it was Michael, not Mike) "is studying to be a photographer – in the *media!*"

By the look of him, Ally thought, *he's studying to be a right poser*. But she didn't say that. Some things you kept to yourself. Cheryl couldn't be provoked indefinitely. And besides, Ally might want a favour from her one day.

"Oh, that's interesting," Ally said. "Fashion photographs?"

"Fashion and weddings and magazine covers. Mostly weddings and babies and passport photographs at the moment. But they reckon he could be the next David Bailey."

"Who reckons?"

"He does."

"And who's David Bailey anyway," Ally said.

"A famous photographer, twerp."

"I've never heard of him."

"No, I don't suppose you would have," Cheryl said.

"But then you haven't got much in the way of culture, have you?"

"Haven't got a vulture?" Ally said, pretending to mishear. "What would I want a vulture for? It would eat the budgie, wouldn't it, and do great big poos all over the carpet."

"*Culture*, not *vulture*, bird-brain! And I'm very surprised you haven't heard of David Bailey. He's photographed the Five Nine. He did their album cover."

"Oh, *did* he?" Ally said. "Did he *really*?"

And she almost got interested in photography then. For about five minutes.

When Cheryl had finished cutting their hair, Pauline went home for an early night and some beauty sleep and to check that she'd packed everything in her bag – just as she had done every day for the last fortnight.

Ally went to show her mum her haircut. She found her in the bedroom, doing her own bit of packing. Her dad wasn't there. He went down to the pub on Fridays to see his mates. He was dead straight though, never took the car and he never came back bad. Well, not *that* bad. Maybe once, one Christmas. But usually you'd not know the difference at all.

"She's done it, Mum. What do you think?"

"Let's see the back." Ally gave her a twirl. "Yes. Nice. Nice cut."

Cheryl stuck her head round the door.

"Mum, would you like me to do yours before I pack away?"

"*Mine?*"

She seemed almost shocked at the idea. She put her hand up to her hair in a defensive gesture. Almost afraid, Ally thought, to want to be pretty any more. But she *was* attractive. Could be, despite being so middle-aged. If she dressed a bit differently, didn't look so tired.

"Mine? Do *my* hair?"

"Why not? You'd going off for the weekend too, aren't you?" Cheryl said.

She was going to say no. You could see it, from the shape of her mouth. But then she changed her mind.

"Okay. I'll be down in a minute."

Cheryl went back downstairs.

"Can I help you, Mum, with the packing?" Ally offered.

"No, it's all done thanks, love."

She sat on the bed. Her mum looked at her.

"We haven't been away for a long time, your dad and me," she said. "A room of our own too. In a hotel. We always shared with you two when we went away before. The last time – you won't believe this – that me and your dad stayed in a hotel in a room on our own, was on our honeymoon."

She seemed to be off somewhere in her mind. Off on

125

some journey she had to make on her own. Ally could never accompany her there. She tried to bring her back to the present.

"Mum. What's Cheryl going to do while we're all up in Birmingham?"

It was those biology lessons. They were preying on her mind. Them and Bruce Willis in his mucky vest with the muscles poking out.

But her mum was still back in the past.

"Yes, before you two were born, it was," she said. "Long time ago. Long, long time ago now."

Ally looked at her mum. She wished she had some of that forty-pounds-a-jar skin revitaliser to give her. She seemed tired and long since run out of youth.

"Mum. What's Cheryl going to do while we're all up in Birmingham?"

"Sorry, love?"

"Cheryl, while we're in Birmingham."

"Oh . . . she's going out with Michael tomorrow night, isn't she?" (The obvious pretence that Cheryl was going to a party with her friend Lyn had by now been dropped.)

"Yes, but I mean, will she be okay, in the house, on her own?" Ally said.

"Oh, I wouldn't worry love, I'm sure she'll be all right."

Oh, come on, Mum. Don't be so slow, Ally thought.

Short of spelling it out in capital letters, what else can I do? You know what I mean!

Mum put a spare pair of socks for Dad into the case.

Take the hint, eh, Mum, Ally willed her. *Take the hint. What I'm trying to say is, are Cheryl and Mike going to be spending the night here together while we're all away up in Birmingham, doing – you know – biology? With a capital B?*

But her mum just went on rolling the socks up and folding up underpants and dropping them into the case.

How can you be so innocent, Mum? How can you not see—

And then it landed on her. The ten ton weight fell on her head.

Mum *did* know. Mum *could* see. Mum was turning a blind eye, giving them her permission. Mum was re-membering. Remembering something in her past, something about her and Dad, something that made her turn that blind eye to Cheryl and Michael. Some-thing that allowed her to understand about them and about Stevie Manns too and the great crush of love.

Something. Only what? Passion, romance? Mum? But Mum and *who*? Dad? Or someone else? Or maybe it *was* Dad. Was that possible? Mum and Dad, a great romance? A great passionate romance, once upon a time? Was that possible? When you got up close and got out the magnify-ing glass, wasn't it the same thing Ally felt for Stevie?

127

But, no, it couldn't be, Ally reasoned. How could it? Nothing could match what she felt for Stevie Manns or what he would one day feel for her. Nothing in the whole history of love.

But then again . . .

Mum, swept off her feet? By Dad? By down-the-pub-every-Friday-two-and-a-half-pints-and-not-a-drop-more-back-by-eleven-fifteen dad? Dad, swept off his feet? By wash-your-hands-the-dinner's-ready-will-you-take-your-boots-off-when-you-come-into-the-house-how-many-times-do-I-have-to-ask-you Mum? Was that possible? Could that once have been? Was it still? In a deep down, dark and cavernous somewhere that you never got a chance to explore?

"*Mum!* Are you *ready?*" Cheryl called from downstairs.

"Just coming!" Mum said.

She went down to get her hair cut. Cheryl was waiting in the kitchen. She always cut their hair in the kitchen. It may not have been the most hygienic of arrangements but the kitchen had a lino floor and that made the cut hair easier to sweep up.

Mum sat on the chair and Cheryl put the towel around her neck to stop the hair getting down inside.

"Washed first?"

"Why not?"

She made Mum get up and go over to the sink.

"Luxury this, a hair wash as well," she said.

"Anyone want any tea?" Ally asked.

Cheryl looked up at her.

"Tea, coffee or orange juice, Ally. That's what we offer them in the salon."

"Tea," said Mum, "will be fine."

Ally put the kettle on. She dropped three teabags into the pot. Her mum would probably have used two. But her head was under the tap and she couldn't see, or prevent, Ally's extravagance.

Ally made the tea. Cheryl towelled Mum's hair from wet to damp, combed it and then began to cut.

"How do you want it?" she said.

"My fate's in your hands," Mum smiled. "So's my head."

"All right."

Cheryl sized up the situation, Chewed her lip a bit, got on the case, just like a female private eye would have done – a *real* female private eye.

"Okay."

She began to cut.

"Are you sure you know what you're doing, Cheryl?" Mum was starting to sound worried. "It feels as if you cut off a really big chunk there."

"It's all right, Mum. Don't worry."

Ally handed round the tea.

"I'll get the dustpan and a brush, shall I?"

"Thanks," Cheryl said. "If you would."

Ally swept up the hair as it fell. It was sad, it was so flecked with grey. She held up the dustpan for them both to see, like she was a surgeon with a bad X-ray, telling a patient that she didn't have long to go.

"Mum, you're getting so *grey!*"

Her mother looked at the contents of the dustpan. She reached out and touched her own greying, cropped hair.

"Yes," she said. "I am, aren't I?"

"Why don't you have a rinse?" Cheryl said.

Mum looked at her as if she'd made an improper suggestion.

"Me? I couldn't. I've never had a rinse. And besides, what would your dad say?"

"Have one, Mum, and find out," Cheryl told her.

So she did.

Cheryl had a selection of rinses in her case. They chose one they thought would be Mum's colour and, when Cheryl had finished cutting, they put it on. Then Cheryl rinsed and dried Mum's hair, using her own professional dryer (that she had bought herself, with her own money, along with her own professional scissors, and you wouldn't *believe* what they'd cost). Ally, meanwhile nipped upstairs to bring down the other mirror so that Mum could see what it looked like at the back.

"I hope you haven't scalped me," she said.

"You'll soon find out," Cheryl said. And she and Ally

exchanged a look, the kind of look they hadn't exchanged for years, since Ally was a little kid and Cheryl was the big sister who'd taken her everywhere and had been happy to do it.

"Okay."

Cheryl took the towel off and held up the mirror. Mum stared at her reflection. Her hand reached slowly up and she touched her hair.

"It's − it's so *different* . . ." she said.

"But do you *like* it?"

"Look at the back, Mum," Ally said. "It's great at the back." And she held up the mirror, wanting Mum to look at the back, to look in the mirror she was holding. The two mirrors she and Cheryl were holding together.

"Yes. Yes. I do like it. I *do*. It's so . . . I look so different. Younger. Do you think I look younger?"

"Years!" Ally said.

"You looked young to start with, Mum," Cheryl said, a bit more tactfully. And she began to put her things away.

"And the colour, that used to be my colour. You know. Years ago back when first met—"

Talk of the devil, of course, and there he was, coming in through the front door, his key rattling in the lock, the door handle turning. Dad's voice called from the hall.

"Anyone up? I'm back!"

If you listened carefully now, you'd hear the rustling

131

of a bag of chips being extracted from an overcoat pocket.

He came into the kitchen. You could smell the pub on him, the beer and the smoke. Not that he did smoke, not for years; but plenty of others did, and the smoke clung to him.

"Just need a bit of ketchup for these—"

Then he saw her. Saw all three of them.

"Cheryl, Ally, you're up late. Where's your—?"

And then he *really* saw her. He nearly dropped his chips.

"Jenny! What – what happened to your—"

He seemed to have forgotten the word. Or he was unable to say it. He just gestured vaguely at his own hair.

"What happened to your – you know—?"

"Cheryl did it for me. For going away. What do you think?"

They all watched him. It was wrong that he had the power to say yes or no, to give the thumbs up or the thumbs down, to destroy or to confirm the beauty of the moment. Yet it wasn't his fault that he had the power. For they had given it to him in wanting his opinion.

"You look . . . wonderful. Beautiful."

And he blushed.

There was a second of silence. A look between them. Looks between everyone. Cheryl and Ally saw the look, and they looked at each other as if to say, "See that. *We* did that. Us and the haircut. We did that."

Then there was the look between Mum and Dad, and the look a moment after that they gave to Cheryl and Ally. It was the look you might give someone when your towel had dropped and they accidentally saw you with nothing on. A look of embarrassment. But also a look of pride and defiance, as if to say that you had nothing to be ashamed of at all, and were just the same as everyone else.

Then the moment had gone. Mum was on her feet and bustling.

"Right. Bed for you, Ally, my girl. Long drive tomorrow. And Cheryl, would you get your dad a plate for those chips, or he'll only drop them everywhere, and—"

"Just a minute, look, just a minute, I mean, you can't just—" Dad protested.

"Can't just what?"

"Can't just – that is – what I meant – what I was going to say was – would anyone like a chip?"

Dad put his open bag of chips down on the table. He motioned at Ally and Cheryl and Mum to come and help themselves.

"Have a chip," he said. "Come on, there's plenty there. Have a chip."

Poor Dad, thought Ally. Poor tongue-tied Dad. He'd been like it ever since she could remember. Ever since she was a little girl.

"Have a chip," he'd say. "Come on, have a chip."
It was his way of saying "I love you."
Have a chip.
She reached out and took one.
"Have a chip," he said. "All have a chip."

9

THE BIG DAY

She'd even forgotten it was her birthday when she opened her eyes that morning. Her mum woke her up, dumping a great heap of cards and presents on her bed.

"What's this for?" Ally said.

"It's your birthday, isn't it? Or have you changed your mind about having one?"

But by then she was already ripping packets open. It made you wonder about the price of wrapping paper. Born to be torn, it was.

"Great, Mum. Thanks. Just what I always wanted. What is it?"

Her mother tried to explain that it was a gadget from the Gadget Shop, but Ally wasn't really taking any of it in. Not the messages on the labels or the good wishes on the cards.

"Be sure to write down who sent what for the thank you letters. Last time you got them mixed up and thanked your Aunt Jean for the bubble bath when she'd sent you a book token."

That was your mother for you. Two seconds after you'd got your presents she was already thinking about thank you letters. Took the gloss off it a bit, that did.

Ally unwrapped a soft parcel and a sweater from the Sweater Shop with *Sweater Shop* written across the front fell out.

"Oh, great, just what I always wanted."

"It's all just what you always wanted, by the sound of it," her mum said.

But it wasn't really. There was only one thing she *really* wanted. And tonight she was going to see him. Stevie Manns all wrapped up in birthday paper and with *Happy Birthday* on the label. That would do just fine.

She got up, got dressed, put on her new sweater, and went down for breakfast. Her dad was already loading up the car.

"What time did you say we'd be round to pick up Pauline?" he asked.

"Half past. But she'll have been ready for hours."

"Well, you'd better get a move on, if you don't want to keep her waiting."

Another suitcase was hauled off in the general direction of the car boot.

"How long are you going for, Dad?" Ally asked. "A fortnight is it, or just the one night?"

"Ask your mother. It's all her stuff, not mine. She'd be taking the kitchen sink if it had handles on it."

Mum came into the kitchen.

"Have you packed your suit?" she said.

"I've even packed the short trousers I used to have when I was ten," her dad answered.

Ally looked up from her muesli.

"What does he want a suit for?"

"We're going to have dinner while you're at the concert."

"Where?"

"At the hotel. Dinner dance. Your dad's got tickets. You *have* got the tickets?"

"No expense spared," he said, and he brandished two tickets at Ally's mum – big ones, the size of postcards.

"Dinner dance?" Ally said. "I didn't know you *could* dance."

"I can't," her dad said. "I'm all right at the dinners though. And your mum can dance, so she can do all the dancing and I can do all the eating. That's known as the perfect partnership."

Ally raised her eyes to the ceiling in a *God help us* look.

"Ignore him," her mum said. "He's trying to be funny."

"Yeah, *trying* being the word," Ally said. "Trying, but not necessarily succeeding."

"Where's your bag, Ally?" her dad asked.

"In the hall."

He took the other suitcase and Ally's bag out to the car and banged the boot lid shut. Her mother fussed around, wiping everything in sight and straightening the tea towel. Her dad came back.

"That's it," he said, watching her mum. "Straighten the tea towels. We wouldn't want any burglars breaking in while we were away and thinking we had untidy tea towels."

Mum gave him a *get knotted* look and put a fresh bin liner into the pedal bin, in case the burglars looked in there as well.

"Anything else to go in the car then?" Dad said. "A sack of sandwiches maybe? A trunk of crisps? A case of biscuits? A few kilos of peppermints? How about the tumble drier and the ironing board?"

"How about you go and put yourself in the car and stop making the kitchen look so untidy," Mum suggested.

"Right," he said. "I will."

They locked up and went out to join him five minutes later. He was in the driver's seat, reading the paper.

"Come on, come on! I don't want to miss the match. I hope your friend Pauline's a bit quicker at getting out of the bathroom than you are."

But Ally just ignored him.

They drove round to Pauline's to find her packed and waiting out by the gate, a card and a birthday present in her hand.

"Happy birthday, Ally!" she said, opening the car

door. "Here you go, Ally!" she handed Ally her present as she got into the back seat next to her. Hello, Mrs Morgan, Mr Morgan."

"Thanks, Pauline."

"All right love?" Ally's dad said, and he put Pauline's luggage in the boot. "Just the one bag, is it? You travel light. Not taking any items of furniture with you then? A couple of sofas and some curtains or anything? You never know when they might come in handy."

The front window went up and Pauline's mum poked her head out. She called to Ally's dad.

"Hello, Hugh."

"Hello, Beryl. All right?"

"Very good of you to take Pauline with you."

"Not at all. Good of her to come."

"Really looking forward to it, she is, he said."

"Aren't we all?"

She spotted Ally's mum then, in the passenger seat.

"All right, Jenny?" And she waved over.

"All right Beryl," Ally's mum waved back. "How's your mother?"

Oh no! Pauline and Ally sat impatiently in the back seat of the car. Ally groaned. If they got into all the *How's your mother?* stuff, they wouldn't get away for hours. They'd be going through the health of each other's next of kin for ages. Then, when they ran out of relatives, it would be *How's the neighbours?* and *How's the cat?* and

How're your toe-nails? and *How are your bowel move-
ments?* and *What did the doctor say?* And, then it would
be who'd died recently and then—

"We'd best get going," Dad said, interrupting them,
no doubt thinking of his football match. Nothing got in
the way of his football. Not even Uncle's Frank's
prostate or Aunt Susan's migraines.

"Have a great time all of you!" Pauline's mum called.

"We will."

"And phone!" Pauline's mum reminded her. "You've
got money for the phone box."

And then they were off. Going, really going at last.

They drove out of Pauline's street and made a left.
Mum was getting the maps out, and Ally could sense an
argument brewing.

"You have to turn right here at the end of the road,"
her mum ordered.

"I'm not going that way," her dad said.

"It's shorter."

"It's more congested though."

"Not on a Saturday."

"*Especially* on a Saturday."

"The lights are changing."

"I can see, I can see."

"You want to concentrate on your driving."

"I could if you'd stop distracting me by talking all the
time!"

140

Ally and Pauline looked at each other and covered their mouths with their hands to stop from laughing. Dad saw them in the rear view mirror.

"And you can stop sniggering and all," he grumbled.

He turned right into Rupert Street. They drove past Marlene Forrester's house and there she was in all her pomp and glory, standing on the doorstep, chatting with Tracey Norris, while Mr Forrester loaded up their car and while her mum just stood there watching, not getting her hands dirty, all dressed up in a big pink hat and gloves halfway up her elbows, as if she was going to a wedding.

Maybe she was – maybe they all were.

Yes, they *were*! That was it. They *must* be. Another *two birds with the one stone* job. Marlene could never have wangled it otherwise. Her dad would never have taken her up to Birmingham just for a Five Nine concert. He spent too much driving anyway, he said, as part of his job, and he wasn't going to start doing it for recreation at the weekends as well.

He had a nice car though. A big, red, sleek thing that his company gave him to drive around in. Still, everyone got stuck in the same traffic jams, no matter how big and sleek their car.

Marlene saw them and they saw her. But they looked right through each other. Mum noticed them as well.

"Hey, look, Ally, there's your friend Marlene."

"*Friend?* You wondered about your parents sometimes. They didn't seem to have a clue about anything. Marlene, a *friend*? It was like calling a man-eating tiger a nice little pussy-cat.

"And your other friend Tracey."

You must *be joking*.

"I wonder where they're going?"

"I think they're going to the concert too, Mrs Morgan," honest Pauline explained.

"Oh, are they? You should have said. We could all have gone up together. All stopped off at the motorway services and had a spot of lunch."

And a jolly little lunchtime that would have been. I don't *think*.

"Turn right here," Ally's mum said, looking at the map.

"I was going to go straight across," her dad said.

"Right's quicker for the motorway."

"If you go straight across, you don't hit the build-up at the roundabout!"

So, by way of compromise, her dad turned left.

"*Now* where are you going?"

"Left! What does it look like!"

"But that takes us back to where we started!"

They'd never get there till the concert was over at this rate.

"Open your present," Pauline said as they drove on. "Aren't you going to?"

142

"Right."

Ally knew it was going to be something to do with the Five Nine and she wasn't wrong. It was a photograph of Stevie. A specially framed one that Pauline must have got from the official fan club, because on the back it said *This Is A Genuine Five Nine Photograph* and at the bottom it was stamped *Official Fan Club*. Which showed you how official it was.

"Thanks, Pauline, that's really great."

Mum turned in her seat, giving the maps a rest for a moment.

"Can I see what you've got?"

Ally held it up.

"It's Stevie."

"Hmm," her mum said, "and we don't see much of *him*, do we?" Then she turned back, thinking of Ally's bedroom, covered in posters of the group, and wondering about all the dust that must be collecting behind them.

She looked round again.

"What're the ceiling and those walls going to look like when you take those posters down, eh? We'll probably have to redecorate."

Take them down? Ally thought. *Take them down? Mum, I'm never going to take them down. So the problem won't arise. If I live to be a hundred, if I never leave home, they'll always be there, eternally young, eternally – Stevie.*

143

"Where're you going to put it?" Pauline asked. "The photograph?"

"Next to my pillow," Ally said. "Under my pillow!" Then she quietly added "Until he *is* my pillow." And she and Pauline giggled.

"Aye, aye," Dad said from the front, "what's the joke now?"

"You have to turn left here," Mum interrupted.

"Of course it's left here," he snapped. "I know that! It's the only way you *can* go."

And then they were on the motorway.

Marlene Forrester's dad overtook them about ten minutes later, his great sleek car breaking the speed limit by at least fifteen miles an hour.

"Oh there's Marlene and Tracey," Mum said. "Aren't you going to wave?"

No, they weren't. Maybe make a few rude hand signals, the sort that weren't in the Highway Code. But wave? No.

"Is it a wedding they're going to first?" Mum asked.

"Her cousin's getting married, I think," Pauline said.

"That'll be nice," Mum said, the way you do.

Ally decided to challenge her. She felt in one of those moods.

"How do you know?" she said.

"Pardon?"

"How do you know it'll be nice, Mum? Her cousin

144

getting married. It might be horrible. It might all be a big mistake."

"You're cheerful," Dad said. "Right little prophet of doom you are. And on your birthday."

"Only asking. It's just everyone says weddings are nice. But are they? That's all. How do we know?"

They approached a sign saying *Services One Mile*.

"Anyone want the toilet?" Mum said.

"Didn't we bring one?" Dad said. "You surprise me. I thought you had one in your bag."

Nobody wanted the toilet.

"I'll go on then," Dad said.

"You *do* go on," Mum murmured.

"Until it's time for something to eat. We'll stop at the services after next."

They drove on. Mum read the paper a while and then fell into a doze, after complaining – as she always did – that reading in cars made her sick. Dad kept up a running commentary about the other drivers on the roads.

"He's going too fast, him. Don't hog the middle lane. Not so close, mate, not so close."

Pauline and Ally looked out of the windows and dreamed.

"Not long now," Pauline said.

"No, not long."

Ally took Mum's newspaper and turned to the music

page. She showed the headline on it to Pauline. *Five Nine To Split Sensation* it read. *Could This Be The Last Time?*

Pauline wasn't impressed.

"They're always saying that," she said. "They've been saying that since they started. There's always rumours and stuff but it's never true. The real fans know that."

Ally nodded her agreement, but she read the article anyway, even if it was treachery.

The rumour is that this time the Five Nine really are set to call it a day, the article began. *The best of friends on stage – backstage, things aren't so rosy. Britain's most successful band, after four years together, now look to be at the end of the road. Harmony has given way to hostility as quarrels over royalty payments and musical direction flare up behind the scenes and in the studio.*

Bobby R is the major songwriter, and as the one who penned all the Five Nine's biggest hits, he also banks the fattest cheques. The other band members have contributed material for the new album to try and even things up a little, but Bobby R now claims that their songs are not up to his standards. (Mr Modesty, eh? Or what?) But what's a song without a singer? And without the voice of Stevie Manns to carry his songs, where would Bobby be today? (Standing in a line at the job centre, perhaps? Maybe someone ought to remind him of that, before his head gets as big as the rest of him?)

146

The band play the last gig of their British tour tonight at the NEC in Birmingham. So if you haven't yet got a ticket then beg, borrow or steal one. Because this could be your last chance to see the Five Nine for a long, long while.

And if they split? What then? Is it back to the nine to five for the Five Nine? Only time can tell.

Ally nudged Pauline and handed her the paper. Pauline read the article but it made no difference to her views.

"It's just journalists," she said. "They're always writing stuff like that. Anything to sell a newspaper." And she handed it back to Ally.

Ally's mum had started to snore. Ally was a bit embarrassed and glanced at Pauline. But Pauline just smiled and said, "My mum's worse. And as for my dad—"

"What's that?" Dad said, ears like a barn owl.

"*Pauline's* dad," Ally explained. "We weren't talking about *you.*"

"Just as well," he said. "I'll not have you two taking my name in vain."

"When'll we get there, Dad?"

"Another hour and a half. I'll stop at the next services first. Okay?"

"Okay, Dad."

"Okay, Pauline?"

"Fine, Mr Morgan. Whatever you say."

"Good."

Pauline went back to staring out of the window. Ally thumbed through the newspaper, working her way from the middle to the front, to—

Suddenly there he *was!*

It was a photograph of Stevie after last night's show, on his way to the after-gig party. The sort of party Marlene (The Monster) Forrester and Tracey (Spit On Her Grave) Norris would be going to tonight.

We was robbed, Pauline, Ally thought, *we was robbed. Robbed on our way to the happiness bank and Marlene Forrester ran off with the takings. Those backstage passes should have been ours.*

Still, no use crying over split milk and rotten cows. Nothing they could do about that now. And at least they'd be seeing the Five Nine on stage, and that was something special in its own right. Even *that* had seemed like an impossible dream, not so long ago.

The photograph which held Ally's attention wasn't just of Stevie alone. No, he was with *her*. That model, Caslile, she was going to the party with him. Her and her totally bogus name.

But Stevie. Stevie and her! Standing so close . . .

Ally's heart wasn't functioning properly. It had

skipped a beat again. It really had. It was an odd, rather frightening sensation. But then it returned to its proper rhythm and she thought that she might live a while longer. Just as long as she lived until the end of tonight's concert. That would do. What came after that wouldn't matter.

But Stevie! Stevie and that *woman!*

Ally didn't want to look at the photograph, and went to turn the page. But she stopped. There was something about the photograph that wasn't quite right. She turned back and made herself look at it again.

Yes. There *was* something wrong. It was in their body language. Instead of holding hands or having their arms round each other like they used to, this time they were just walking side by side. And their faces were turned away. Or rather hers was turned away from his. But he was still looking at her, glancing at her sideways, almost – hopefully, as if to say *What's the matter?* kind of thing. *You okay? What's up? What have I done?* Or *What* haven't *I done?* But she wasn't having any of it and just kept her eyes straight ahead, as though she was with him, but wasn't really with him at all.

Stevie? What was going on?

Ally nudged Pauline.

"Pauline. Look." She showed her the photograph.

"Oh yeah," Pauline said. "Stevie and Gladys." She didn't make any further comment though and leafed through the newspaper, looking for photographs of Charlie.

"They haven't got a photo of Charlie, have they?" she asked.

"No. Not this time," Ally said. "He was in yesterday."

"Oh."

Pauline lost interest and went to give her the paper back, but Ally nudged her again.

"No, but look Pauline, at the photo, I mean what do you *think*?"

She held the newspaper up for her to see.

"About what?"

"About *them*?" Pauline wasn't half slow on the uptake sometimes.

"What about them?" Pauline said.

"How it is *between* them, of course!"

Pauline studied the photograph.

"Well, you can't say she's not good-looking, that Caslile. I suppose most blokes would think she was gorgeous. Someone should flatten her with a tractor," she added.

"But look, Pauline, don't you see? They're not *looking* at each other. What could that mean?"

"Means they weren't looking at each other, Ally. You can't be looking at each other and holding hands and that lovey-dovey stuff *all* the time. They have to go to the toilet and things you, know, same as the rest of us. You can't be holding hands in there. You can take together-ness *too* far."

"But they took this photo on the way into the party, Pauline, not on the way into the loo. When you're going into a party, you should look happy and pleased to be with someone, shouldn't you?"

"Yeah but you know how they take those photo-graphs, Ally. I mean, those photographers aren't exactly *wanted*, are they? All hanging round club doors, sticking their cameras in your face, bouncers pushing them out the way and that. I mean, these celebrities and so on, they aren't exactly queuing up to say cheese and watch the birdie, are they? It's just a bad photograph, that's all."

Ally didn't pursue the matter any further, but she had a different view on that photograph. Something was not quite right.

The trouble was that although Pauline *was* a true Five Nine fan, she was more of a Charlie fan than a Stevie fan, which left her a bit blinkered, and so she didn't *know* Stevie the way Ally knew him. She wasn't aware of the nuances of his moods, his highs and lows, his light and shade. But Ally could tell from the photograph that all was *not* right. Not right at all between Stevie and Caslile.

The truly weird thing about the photo was the way in which he was looking at Caslile. Appealingly, almost. The way you'd look at someone who'd just told you they were packing you in, when you were still madly in love with them and when you were trying to salvage a bit of pride, though what you really felt like doing was begging them not to leave you, as you cried all over their shoes.

Yet *he* was like that. Not her, *him!* Stevie, with all those thousands of girls in love with him. *He* looked like the one who was hurt. *He* looked rejected, the one no longer wanted. *Him*. Not *her*. Just like in the lyrics to *Look Back As You Go*.

Look back as you go
Turn and see me cry
Watch and walk away
All the times we tried.

You will never know
How I feel for you,
How I hoped and prayed
Never been so blue
So look back as you go.

Ally's heart skipped another beat. But this time it didn't frighten her. It seemed to make her feel stronger, more alive.

If Stevie Manns was going to split up with Caslile, well, then he'd be vulnerable, and in need of comfort and a true, sympathetic shoulder on which to cry.

And Ally would be there for him. If only he knew that. If only she could get a message to him somehow and let him know. If only he realised that Ally was there for him, ready and waiting. If he was unhappy, if his heart was broken, if he was hurt and sad, she would be there for him, to bandage his wounds.

Always and forever
More and more and now
Somehow, somewhere, someday
Keep that precious vow.

"Stevie, I'm here for you. You only ever need to ask!"

Her dad looked at her in the rear view mirror.

"Eh? What's that you said, Ally?"

Ally blushed purple. Had she said it out loud?

"Nothing, Dad, nothing, just muttering. Singing, that's all."

"Wake your mum up, will you? We're nearly at the services."

Ally shook her mum. She noticed that Pauline was asleep as well and she prodded her awake too.

"Pauline!" she said. "Break!"

They stopped at the services and had an early lunch. There was no sign of Marlene Forrester lurking about anywhere like a big germ, and within half an hour they were on their way.

"I'll drop you off at the hotel first and then you can amuse yourselves for the afternoon while I get to the football. You can maybe go down to the Bull Ring, if you like," Ally's dad said.

Pauline looked blank.

"Bullring, Mr Morgan?" she said. "In Birmingham? Bullfighting in Birmingham? I thought they only did that in Spain. Anyway, it's cruel. I don't want to see bullfighting."

"No, no, it's a name for part of the city," Ally's dad said. "You can do a bit of shopping round there, I think. It's not a real bullring any more than Spaghetti Junction's real spaghetti."

"Ah," said Pauline. "Right."

Dad looked at her in the rear view mirror.

"Haven't you been to Birmingham before, Pauline?"

"I haven't been hardly *anywhere* before, Mr Morgan," said Pauline. "We don't really go on trips and things much. My mum's got a phobia."

"What, about going outside the house?"

"No," Pauline answered, "about my dad's driving."

Ally's mum was awake and back at the maps.

"Next exit," she instructed.

"I know," Dad told her.

"As long as you do," she said.

"Dad," Ally said, as they drove the last few miles. "Is the hotel near the concert place, the NEC?"

"Near as I could get."

"Good."

"Be there any moment."

"Right."

"Left here," Mum said.

154

"Are you sure?"

"Of course I'm sure. If you don't like my directions, how about I drive then and you hold the map."

"Okay. And then *I* can criticise *you*."

"Now, now, you two!" Ally said. "Children, children!"

Finally they turned off into the slip-road that led to the hotel.

"What the—?!!"

Dad stood on the brakes.

"What is it, Dad? An accident?"

"I don't know. But it's definitely something."

Pauline and Ally pressed their noses to the car windows.

"What is it? What's going on?"

There were hundreds – no, *thousands* of them – all milling around in front of the hotel. Thousands of them, nearly all of them girls. Some of them were in noisy crowds, singing songs at the tops of their voices. Others were just standing there crying. Others stood expressionless, as if they had no emotion in them at all. Zombified, as if their brains had been sucked out by a vacuum cleaner.

By the side of the slip-road, a girl who had fainted in the crush was lying on a stretcher and being looked after by a St John's Ambulance lady. There was also a regular hospital ambulance in attendance, along with two or three police cars and a couple of riot vans.

Dad wound his window down as a policeman came over towards their car.

"Sorry, sir," the policeman said. "I'm afraid you can't come in here."

"What do you mean, can't come in here?" Dad said. He wasn't a man to be intimidated by uniforms. "We're stopping here the night. We've got a reservation. Two rooms booked. Weeks ago."

"Ah, I see," the policeman said. "Then that's a bit different. Okay. Just hang on a minute and we'll see if we can clear your way." He called to some of his colleagues.

"Help me clear a path, will you?" he said. "See this gentleman through." Then he returned to the car.

"Drive very slowly would you, please, sir. We don't want anyone crushed."

"No. Right you are," Dad said. "I'll be careful."

"Be sure to drive slowly," Mum repeated.

"I heard what he said!"

They had to wait a minute while the police cleared a path for them to drive up to the front of the hotel.

Ally and Pauline sat in the back of the car, smiling as though they had gone to heaven.

"Are you thinking what I'm thinking?" Ally asked.

"Yes," said Pauline, "I am. Must be!"

"Has to be," said Ally. "No other way!"

And she was right. *The Five Nine were staying in the hotel.* The policeman told them that they had taken over the penthouse suite. They were all there, *all* of them.

Ally's eyes sparkled. Who'd ever have *believed* it, *thought* of it, *imagined* it! She had pictured so many other impossible things, but she'd never even dared to dream of this. She reached and took Pauline's hand and gave it a squeeze.

"Stevie!" she whispered.

"Charlie!" Pauline said.

And outside clusters of girls were shouting and chanting the same words.

"Stevie, Stevie, we want Stevie!"

"Charlie, Charlie, where are you, Charlie!"

"Nitz, Nitz, we love you to bitz!"

"We love Bobby, we love Bobby," some girls were chanting. "He looks like Mr Blobby, but we love Bobby!"

And Ally and Pauline collapsed with laughter.

Dad edged the car towards the entrance. Suddenly the crowd surged forward and out of his way, heading for the east side of the hotel and leaving him a clear run.

Up at the penthouse suite a window had opened and a face was looking down.

"It's Nitz," said Ally. "*Look!*"

He was peering down at the mob and puffing on a cigarette. He finished the cigarette, crushed it out on the window ledge, and flicked the stub down.

"It's mine!" a girl screamed. "It's mine, mine!"

She and a hundred others all ran at once to get the

stub. It fell to the ground. A girl reached for it. So did another and another. Someone was pushed, someone fell. Soon there was a mass of seething bodies on the ground, and frightened voices shouting, "Get off me! Help, help, I can't breathe!"

Then the police and the ambulance men were in among them, pulling them off each other.

Mum watched the incident from the car.

"You know," she said, "I'm having second thoughts about this concert."

"Oh, Mum, it's not like that at the concert. It's all seats and security men."

"I hope so."

The police had more or less sorted it out now. Two girls remained, the ones who had been at the bottom of the heap. They sat up, both holding on to Nitz's discarded cigarette stub with torn fingernails.

"*I got it!*"

"*I got it!*"

And neither of them would let go.

"Give it to me," a policeman said. They reluctantly handed it over. He tore the cigarette butt in two, and gave them back a half each.

"There," he said, "now you've *both* got it, okay?"

And that was the long arm of the law for you.

They got to the parking bay outside of the hotel

reception then. The one marked *Unloading Only* in yellow asphalt.

The police cleared a path for them to get to the hotel door.

"Okay, let the people in, please, let the people in!"

They even gave Dad a hand with the suitcases.

"Who are you?" a girl shouted to them as they went in. "Are you famous?"

"Don't be daft!" Ally's mum said. "Do we look famous?"

Then they were inside, in the cool air-conditioned lobby of the hotel.

"Mr and Mrs Morgan and daughter and friend," Dad was saying to the receptionist. "We booked adjoining rooms."

"Oh yes, sir, here you are."

Dad filled in the necessary forms and the receptionist handed him the room keys.

"The porter will help you with your luggage if you can wait a—"

"That's all right, we'll manage." He wasn't tipping any porters if he didn't have to. Not Dad.

"Then it's up on the fifteenth floor, rooms fifteen-twelve and fifteen-fourteen. The lift's—"

"I can see it. Thank you. Come on."

They loaded the luggage on to a trolley and headed for the lift.

159

As they stood in the lift, Ally looked at the buttons. They went up to fifteen and then there was the letter P for the penthouse, then R for roof gardens. The policeman had said that the Five Nine had taken the penthouse over. That meant that the band were directly above them. Directly above them. Stevie would be just above her. Maybe even in the *room* above her. Stevie, Stevie Manns, no more than a few feet away. So close you could almost reach out and touch.

It was the best birthday present ever.

10

SO NEAR AND YET SO FAR

It was going to be a whole load of skin off Marlene Forrester's nose, that was for certain. Because maybe she and Tracey Norris did have backstage passes and tickets for the party after, but they didn't have the greatest band in the entire world living just above their heads.

"Maybe we could knock a hole in the ceiling, and climb up?" Pauline suggested. "Or use the beds as trampolines?"

"I don't think the hotel would like that too much."

"Be worth it though," Pauline said.

And Ally was almost tempted.

They were unpacking in their room, room fifteen-twelve. Ally's mum and dad were next door in fifteen-fourteen doing same.

"Hey, look at this," Pauline shouted from the bathroom. "Free dressing gowns!"

She came in, trying one on on top of her clothes.

"Smart, eh? Have you ever seen anything so white? Almost like an ad for soap powder. Do you think you get to take them home?"

Ally handed her a small card which was sitting on top of the dressing table *Bath robes are for use in the room and pool area only*, it read. *Patrons wishing to purchase souvenir bath robes may do so from reception. Price £60.*

"Sixty quid!" Pauline said indignantly. "For a bit of old towel. Stuff that!"

But she left the robe on and went to see what else was provided.

"What's this?" she said, finding something.

"The trouser press, isn't it?" Ally said.

"Wish I'd brought some trousers. I could have pressed them."

Ally continued unpacking. She set out the clothes she was going to wear to the concert that night.

"Hey look," Pauline said, "I've found a kettle. And a basket of stuff. Tea, coffee, hot chocolate, cream, sugar, artificial sweetener, biscuits—"

"Biscuits!"

They ate the biscuits. Then Pauline found the fridge.

"Hey, look at this," she said, opening up the fridge to reveal a small Aladdin's cave of sparkling bottles. "It's full of booze." She took something out. "Champagne! And chocolate. And peanuts. And coke. And mineral water."

"Price list!" Ally added, finding a piece of paper on the top of the fridge, listing its contents and what they cost. She passed it to Pauline.

"Stone the flipping crows," she said. "All that for a coke? And they're only little bottles!" She slammed the door shut. "I'm not having any of that. Let's have a cup of hot chocolate instead. At least it's free."

Pauline went and put the kettle on and made some hot chocolate from the complimentary sachets. Neither of them really wanted any, but it was free, and they were in a hotel room, where you had your own kettle, and so they had some anyway, because it was different.

Pauline put the TV on.

"Look at this," she said. "They've got satellite."

"And an in-hotel movie," Ally said.

"*And* an adult channel!" Pauline said. "Let's have a look at the adult channel."

But – like the drinks in the fridge – the adult channel had to be paid for. So they didn't bother.

Ally flicked through all the free channels with the remote control. It seemed to be sport on most of them, and football at that. Football, the most boring game in the world. How could anyone get passionate about football? Get passionate about Stevie Manns, yes. But football, it was just so dull.

Some girls liked it though. Even her sister Cheryl went to matches now and again and claimed to enjoy them. Ally reckoned she only went to keep Mike company. Mum never went with Dad. She hated the game too.

"I'd rather watch paint dry," she'd say. "I'd rather watch water get wet."

"You," Dad would say, "are football-illiterate."

"I'd rather be football-illiterate than football-stupid," Mum answered once, and he sort of dropped the subject after that.

Cheryl and Mike – Ally had forgotten about them. And what would *they* be doing later, with the house to themselves, eh? B.I.O.L.O.G.Y., that's what.

They should try chanting that at football matches:

"Whadda we want?

Biology!

When do we want it?

Now!"

That might make Match of the Day a bit more interesting.

Ally looked at the digital radio-clock set between the two beds. You could programme it to wake you up in the morning – if you could understand the instructions.

Pauline had found her way back into the bathroom.

"Hey, Ally, there's baskets of stuff in here too," she called. "Shower gel, shampoo, moisturiser, soap, all in little pots. Oh, and look at this. What's this?"

She came out, trailing paper.

"I think," said Ally, "that it's a paper toilet seat cover."

Pauline looked at it – critical, but impressed.

"They've got it all here, haven't they? I think I might

164

take some of that shower stuff home. Do you think that's all right?"

"Probably," Ally said. "As long as you don't take *too* much. They probably expect you to take *some* of it."

She finished hanging her clothes up and took a sip of her hot chocolate.

"I must hang my things up too," Pauline said. She unpacked her case and got out her clothes for the evening.

"So what now?" she said, when she had done. "Hours to kill yet. How shall we murder them?"

And as if to answer her, the telephone rang.

They both sat looking at it.

"Do you think that's for us?" Pauline said.

"Well, it's ringing in our room," Ally pointed out.

"But who knows we're here?"

"Maybe it's a wrong number."

"Maybe it's a funny phone call."

"Do you think we should answer it?"

"Maybe it's your mum and dad."

"Yeah, probably."

"Yeah, or maybe," Pauline said, "it's from upstairs."

"Upstairs?" Ally said. "What do you mean?"

"Upstairs," Pauline repeated. "You know, the band. Maybe they were looking out of the window and saw us coming into the hotel. Maybe they thought, *who are those stunningly attractive girls with the obviously amazing personalities?* And they rang down to reception to get

165

our room number, and now they're ringing to invite us up to the penthouse for –" she faltered "– for a cup of hot chocolate or something!"

Ally didn't think it likely. But all the same, you never knew. What if it *was* Stevie Manns ringing down? Stevie ringing and she didn't answer—

They both made a grab for the phone at once, but it had already stopped.

"Ah!"

"Drat!"

A few seconds later, there was a knock at the door. *It's him*, Ally thought, and her mouth went dry, *it's really him*. And in a trance, she went to open the door.

But it wasn't him at all. It was just her dad.

"What's up with you two, have you got cloth ears?" he said. "I was ringing you from next door. I could hear the phone through the wall. Why didn't you answer it?"

"Sorry, Dad. We thought it was maybe a wrong number. You know, not having stayed in a hotel before."

"Yeah, well, I'm off to the football then," he said. "And your mum's going in to the centre to look at the shops. Do you want to go in with her, or are you stopping here?"

There was – there could be – only one answer.

"We'll stay here, Mr Morgan, if that's all right," Pauline said.

"Stay here, Dad, I think, yeah."

"Yeah, I thought you might. And what are you going

166

to do? Not just moon about making a nuisance of yourselves?"

"Maybe we'll go and have a swim, Mr Morgan."

"Yeah," Ally agreed. "In the hotel pool."

"Did you bring your cossies?"

"Yes, Mr Morgan."

"Yes, Dad."

"All right. Well, here's a fiver for a cup of coffee and a cake. Back about sixish. I'll see you then. And stay out of trouble."

"Okay, Dad."

"Thanks, Mr Morgan."

"Enjoy the match, Dad."

"Bye."

Mum came out of the room next door and met Dad in the corridor as he was returning to fifteen-fourteen.

"They say they're staying here," he told her.

"Think they'll be all right on their own?"

"Yeah. You've got to trust kids on their own at some point and they're sensible enough."

And of course Ally and Pauline *were* sensible. Sensible, responsible, but ever so slightly mad.

Ally's mum and dad said cheerio to the girls before they went.

"Okay, see you later, you two."

"Bye Mum."

"Bye Mrs Morgan."

"Have a good time."

And they were off, down in the lift, Ally's dad with his supporter's scarf wound round his neck, her mum clutching her shopping list.

"Good!" Ally said. "They've gone."

"Right."

"Let's get planning."

"Right."

Ally paused a moment. "Listen," she said. "It doesn't stop, does it?"

She meant the sound from outside. The voices chanting, "Stevie, Stevie, we love you, Stevie," and "Nitz, Nitz, we love you to bitz!", punctuated by odd screams and short-lived outbursts of hysteria. Sometimes a police or an ambulance siren wailed its departure or its arrival.

"Just think," Ally said, "*they're* out *there*."

"Yes," said Pauline smugly "And *we're* in *here*." And she pointed at the ceiling above her head. "With *them*! Just up *there*!"

"And only a bit of wood and plaster between us."

Surely, Ally thought, if love could conquer everything, it could conquer a bit of wood and plaster. It could conquer a ceiling.

Couldn't it?

Pauline took her hotel dressing gown and found a thick bath towel, and then rolled up her swimming costume inside it. They'd known there was going to be a pool. Ally's dad had told them, several times.

"There's a pool in this hotel. Free to residents," he'd said. "All included in the price. So we might as well take advantage of it."

He was great on taking advantage of what was included. He'd probably eat so much breakfast tomorrow morning, it would be coming out of his ears, and he'd tell everyone else to do the same.

"Have another loaf of toast, there, Ally. It's all included. Have another six pints of orange juice, Pauline. Here, get another twelve poached eggs and a couple more plates of bacon down you. It's a long time till lunch. Come on."

Ally found herself cringing with embarrassment and it hadn't even happened yet.

Pauline sat on her bed while Ally got her swimming things ready.

"So," she said. "How do we get up there? Have we got a plan? Or do we just wing it?"

"Wing it," Ally said.

"Right. Let's get winging, and find out what we can."

They took their swimming stuff and dressing gowns, picked up their room key, and went out to get the lift.

"Where is it?" Pauline said. "The pool?"

"In the basement," Ally said. But instead of punching the B button at the bottom of the line, she punched the P button near to the top. P for Penthouse.

"What are you doing?" Pauline said. "What are you *doing!*"

"Winging it," Ally explained. "Like we said." And the lift went up to the penthouse.

It was there in a second. The doors opened. But there seemed to be something blocking the light. It was a huge bouncer in a lounge suit. He must have been the biggest man Ally had ever seen.

"Yes, ladies? Can I help you?"

"Er . . . is this where the swimming pool is?"

"No, ladies. The swimming pool is down in the basement."

"Are you sure it isn't up here?" Pauline said, all innocent. "Can we come in and have a look around? We might be able to find it."

"Take my word for it," the bouncer said grimly. "It isn't here. But if it turns up I'll let you know. So, nice try, but cheerio. Going – down!"

He leant inside the lift and pressed the B for basement button. The doors began to close. They tried to get a glimpse of what was behind the security man, but his bulk filled the door. It was like trying to peer through a blocked up key-hole.

"See anyone?" Pauline asked Ally, as they descended.

"No. Just Mr Muscles."

"Nor me." Pauline looked a bit downcast, but

instantly brightened up. "Maybe," she said, "they're having a swim. All that keep fit, they've got to do it somewhere. Maybe they're down in the pool!"

But the group weren't having a swim. Or a sauna. Or a Jacuzzi. Or a sit down in the steam room. Or a ride on the cycling machine. Or a row on the rowing machine. Or a dip in the freezing cold plunge bath. Or drinking a coke at the pool-side bar. Or anything, anywhere. They just weren't around.

"Has anyone from the Five Nine been down?" Pauline asked the pool attendant, with as much indifference as she could muster. Whether they'd been in, or whether they hadn't, her tone seemed to say, it was all the same to her.

"Yeah, they were all down actually, earlier on," he said.

Ally nearly dropped her towel.

"They *were*? There were actually *here*? You mean, in the *water*? The same water that we're going in? This very water *here*?"

The pool attendant – whose name was Jeff, according to the name badge on his vest – gave her a funny look.

"Yeah," he said. "Well, they weren't swimming in the sink. They had the whole place to themselves for an hour. Closed it to the residents. Must have cost. Still, money's no object to them, is it?"

"So you mean, do you?" said Pauline, that *you* were actually here at the same time? *You* were actually standing *here* when the Five Nine came in?"

"Well, not standing exactly *here*. I didn't draw stencils round me feet or anything. But standing somewhere in the vicinity, yeah. I have to be on duty, you see, I'm the attendant. It's in case someone gets into difficulties in the pool."

"And did anyone? Get into difficulties?" Ally asked.

"No."

"And so did you speak to any of them?" Pauline said.

"Yeah, I suppose."

"Which one?" she wanted to know.

"A couple of them."

"Stevie?" Ally said.

"Charlie?" Pauline asked.

"Nitz?"

"Bobby R?"

Jeff was thinking. Finally, "The tall one," he said. "I talked to the tall one."

Pauline practically squealed.

"Charlie! You talked to *Charlie!*" She shook Ally by the arm. "Ally, he talked to Charlie!" She turned back to Jeff. "What a fascinating life you must have," she said, "down here by the swimming pool."

"And the other one I talked to," Jeff said (not looking as though life by the swimming pool was *all* that fascinating) "was that one with a bit of a beard."

It was Ally's turn to swoon.

"Stevie!" she cried. "You talked to *Stevie!*"

"Did I?" Jeff the pool attendant said. "Well, if that's who he was, I suppose I did."

Ally stared at him in wonder. He had seemed quite ordinary up till then, but now he took on a kind of spiritual aura. He almost seemed to glow.

"You talked to *Stevie!* And what did he *say?*"

"What did he say?" Jeff scratched his head. "About what?"

"About *anything!*" Ally nearly screeched.

"Oh," Jeff mumbled. "Now let me think." He stroked his chin with his thumb. "Yeah, I remember. He asked me for a towel. He said: 'Have you got a spare towel, mate? I've left mine up in my room.' "

Have you got a spare towel, mate? I've left mine up in my room.

Of course, yes, that was just the sort of thing Stevie *would* say. It was so *him*. So *Stevie*. Trying to be normal, putting everyone at their ease.

"And what about Charlie, the tall one, did *he* say anything?" Pauline asked.

"Yeah, he did," Jeff remembered. It was all coming back to him now. "He said, 'Have you got a towel for me too, chief. I've left mine up in my room as well.' "

"So what did you do?" Ally asked, excitedly.

"Well, I gave them both a couple of towels," Jeff said. "And the tall one, he said, 'Cheers, mate.' "

" 'Cheers mate'? He said 'Cheers mate'? Charlie said that?" Pauline asked.

"And what about Stevie? What did *he* say?" Ally demanded. "When you gave him a towel?"

Jeff looked bemused. He had never known himself to be so much the centre of attention before. Fame was a truly amazing thing.

"I think he said 'Cheers mate,' as well."

"Anything else?"

"Yeah, then one of the other two, that one with the tattoos –" (it must have been Nitz) "– He said, 'It's hot in that sauna, isn't it?' And I said, 'It's supposed to be.' And the one who's a bit tubby" (Bobby R, who else?) "– he said . . . no, I can't remember what he said . . . yes, I do! He asked if we sold swimming goggles. And I said yes. So he bought a pair."

"Anything else," Ally said, "that you remember them saying? Especially Stevie."

"And Charlie?" Pauline added.

"No, not really. They just did a bit of swimming and larking about. And their manager was down here as well, and a couple of their roadies. No. Nothing to stick in the mind. No, they were just sort of enjoying the facilities, really and I let them get on with it. Though when they were leaving, they did call through from the changing room to say they were going. And that Stevie one, I think it was, he said, 'Thanks a lot mate. We're off now.' And the Charlie one, he said. 'See you.' And that was it."

"Well, thank you," Ally said. "Thank you very much."

"Yes, thanks a lot," Pauline said.

"We're going to have a swim now," Ally said. "In the very same water that Stevie and Charlie swam in. It still *is* the same water, isn't it?"

"It is as far as I know," Jeff said. "I certainly haven't changed it."

So Ally and Pauline splashed around for a while, but they were too distracted to do any serious swimming. They got out of the pool after ten minutes and went back up to their room.

"To think," Ally said, as they sat on their beds, "that I was in the same pool as Stevie. We shared the same chlorine! Me and Stevie. It's so . . . I don't know . . . *personal*. Don't you think, Pauly? So, almost . . . *intimate*."

Pauline nodded. "Same for me and Charlie," she said. "It's almost as if we had a bath together."

They sat in silence for a while, savouring their thoughts. Pauline looked at the radio clock. "Still hours to the concert," she said. "What'll we do now?"

"I know," Ally said. She sat bolt upright. "The fire escape!"

"The *what?*"

"Fire escape!"

"*Fire escape!*"

"Yes," said Ally. "The fire stairs. They don't just go *down*, do they? They go *up* as well? All the way to the penthouse."

"You're right," Pauline said. "You're absolutely right."

Ten minutes later, they had changed out of their swimming costumes, dried their hair, and were ready to go.

"My eyes are red from the chlorine," Pauline said. "I look as if I've been crying."

"Don't worry about it, you'll be weeping buckets at the concert anyway," Ally pointed out.

"True enough," Pauline said. "Let's go."

They left the room, walked past the lift, and headed towards the end of the corridor, where an illuminated sign spelt out *EXIT* in red neon.

Fortunately the door to the emergency stairwell wasn't alarmed. They pushed it open and found themselves in a chilly, functional, cold concrete stairwell – an abrupt contrast to the warmth and plush elegance of the carpeted hall.

"Up," Pauline said. And up they went. They turned a corner and came to another door.

"This must be it then. Penthouse again. The other way in. Tradesman's entrance."

"Right. Here we go."

Ally gingerly pushed open the door.

Another shadow. Another immense figure blocking the light. More security in a suit.

"Yes, ladies, can I help you?" the bouncer asked, polite but firm. The Five Nine had bouncers everywhere, on every door.

"Oh, hello. Is this the roof gardens?" Ally said, doing her scatty schoolgirl act, her *I-know-I'm-thick-but-I-can't-help-it* impression.

He wasn't taken in though.

"No, ladies," he said, "this is the penthouse. The roof gardens are up there." And he jerked a thumb in the direction of the stairs.

"Oh, sorry to bother you then," Ally said. "Thanks very much. We're just getting so scatty, aren't we Doreen?" she said to Pauline.

"We are, Mavis," Pauline said. "We'd forget our heads if they weren't kept on with Blu Tac."

Then they did the *girlies-with-the-giggles* bit, for the sake of authenticity. The bouncer refused to crack a smile though. He closed the door in their faces and they were back in the stairwell. From behind the door they heard voices.

"Who was that?" someone said.

"Fans. Try anything, won't they?"

Followed by chuckles of amusement.

"Ha, flipping ha!" Pauline said. "Callous lot those bouncers. I bet they weren't Charlie's idea."

"Or Stevie's," Ally said, springing to his defence. "He wants to *meet* his fans. Not be kept away from them at arm's length. He said so in that interview in *Dream Magazine*."

"Hang on," Pauline said. "Roof gardens. Let's go up."

"Eh?" said Ally. "What for?"

"See what we can see. Come on."

They went on up the fire stairs and came to a door to the roof. A sign on it said: *NO ENTRY. ROOF GARDENS CLOSED*. But the door didn't seem to be alarmed, so they pushed it open.

"What now?" Ally said.

"Have a look."

"Careful."

A high parapet surrounded the roof gardens. They peeked over it, down at the crowd of fans surrounding the hotel. They were still chanting and singing and screaming and crying and fainting and being taken away in ambulances and held back by the police.

"Bobby, I *love* you!" a lone, piercing voice wailed.

"Not as much as *I* do!" a second voice called.

"I love you more than both of them put together!" a third cried.

Up on the roof, Ally and Pauline felt themselves superior to it and above it all. Privileged, advantaged – almost as if they had backstage passes and party invitations for after.

"Makes you feel sorry for them really," Pauline said. "Crying their little hearts out."

"Stevie, Stevie wave to me, Stevie!" an anguished voice cried from way below. Its plaintive appeal was followed by a long series of sobs.

"Poor things," Ally agreed, looking down at the mob.

The wind blew and whistled over the roof gardens. The loungers were stacked up in a heap and their cushions were locked away somewhere. The bar was shuttered and dirty where muddy rainwater had dripped and dried upon it.

"Come on, I'm getting cold, let's go," Pauline shivered. She should have brought a sweater or something.

They walked back towards the door. As they crossed the roof, they stepped over a section of thick mottled glass, which had been set into the roof to allow some natural light to enter into the penthouse corridor below.

"Wait, look!" Ally crouched down. "Look, Pauline. You can see down into it."

They both knelt around the perimeter of the glass so that their shapes could not be spotted from beneath, and they peered down inside. They could discern vague shapes – distorted by the thickness of the glass – moving about in the corridor beneath, going from one room to another.

"See anyone?"

"There's that bouncer, the one who was by the lift."

He came and went, his bulk unmistakable, even through the distortion of the glass.

"If you crinkle your eyes up," Pauline said, "You can see the shapes better. They make more sense."

They crinkled their eyes and looked down. It worked quite well. It was like looking at one of those hidden identity shots on the TV news or in the fly-on-the-wall documentaries. If you screwed up your eyes when you looked at them, you could often make out the real image quite well.

"Ally, here's someone now."

And there he was. There he honestly, really, truly was. Stevie. It was *him*. Crossing from somewhere to some-where. A bedroom to a kitchen, maybe, a living room to a bathroom. She was looking down on him, on his unmistakable haircut . . .

"Stevie – it's *Stevie!*" She could hardly breathe.

If only she could hear what he was saying, but the glass was too thick.

He was gone, as suddenly as he had appeared.

"Maybe he'll come back," Ally said. "Let's stay a bit."

"Maybe we'll see Charlie!" Pauline said, her voice full of hope, her teeth chattering.

They must have stayed there for another forty minutes, getting colder and colder, until finally, on the verge of hypothermia, Pauline said, "It's no good, Ally, I'm getting so cold, I'll need one of those aluminium survival blankets in a minute. And we've got to get changed for the concert soon. And I dare

180

say your mum and dad will be back and they'll be wondering."

"Okay," said Ally, "I suppose we ought to go."

And she realised that she was shivering too.

"I'm sorry," she added, "that you didn't see Charlie."

"Me too," Pauline said. "But never mind. I'll see him tonight."

Yes, she would see Charlie, Ally thought, but not from this close. Not from just a few feet away. Not as near as Ally had been to Stevie just then. Right there, no more than twelve feet away. Stevie. Her Stevie. The one and only Stevie.

She had shared his swimming pool. (All right, so he hadn't been in it at the time. But it was still sharing of a sort. It was just consecutive sharing rather than simultaneous sharing, but it was sharing all the same.) And now she had seen the top of his head.

They were getting closer and closer. Surely they *had* to meet, surely it was *meant* to be. You dipped your pen in moonlight and wrote it in the stars for all the planets in the universe to see.

No, she couldn't give up hope now. She had got this far and destiny had been with her at every step. Its guiding hand had seen to it that she went to the NEC concert in Birmingham and not the one in London. Its intervention had made sure that they stayed at *this* hotel and not one of many others her dad might have chosen.

Now she was here, and *he* was here, and all they had to do was to meet. There *had* to be a way. There *must* be. There had to be a way to meet him before the day was over. She knew that this was the greatest chance of her life, and it would never come again.

Not half way to paradise any more, but *all* the way to heaven.

11

COUNT DOWN

They met Ally's dad in the corridor as they returned to their room. Judging by his demeanour and the jaunty way he had tied his scarf round his neck, his team must have won.

"Where have you two been?" he said. "Exploring? Did you go to the pool?"

"We were up on the roof," Ally said. "Looking at the roof gardens. They're closed really. It's too cold."

"Up on the roof?" he said. "Sounds like a good title for a song."

A song which Ally's dad unfortunately decided to burst into, complete with dance routine and gestures. He only knew half the words though, if that. Remembering tunes and lyrics was never his strong point.

"When this old world is getting me down," he bellowed, "do do do dee doo," he improvised, "up on the roo-oooof!"

He sounded like closing time on a Saturday night. Talk about embarrassing.

Ally's mum stepped out of the lift just then, clutching

four or five carrier bags. She stopped to witness the exhibition Ally's dad was making of himself and she looked about as embarrassed as Ally felt. As for Pauline, she was sort of lingering at a distance back down the corridor, inspecting the ice-making machine as though it was one of the world's seven wonders.

"Hughbert," Ally's mum said, (she always called him Hughbert when it was trouble), "Put a sock in it, will you?"

He stopped, turned, and looked at her.

"You're back," he smiled. Then he looked at the bags. "And you've been spending money. Now *that's* what I like to see."

He searched in his pockets for the room key.

"I take it they won then, Dad?" Ally said.

"What do you reckon?" he grinned. And he winked, and went into another toe-curling, blood-curdling chorus of *Up on the roo-oooof!* croaking like a frog with a bad throat. Then he paused.

"Now who was it who recorded that?" he said. "*Up On The Roof*? Was it Sam Cooke or was it the Drifters?"

Pauline looked up from the ice-maker.

"The Five Nine do a great version of it, Mr Morgan, on their *Dance Forever, Love Forever* CD."

"*Do* they," Ally's dad said. "*Do* they now indeed." Ally began to wonder if he hadn't had a couple of beers to celebrate his team's win on the way home. "Not as good as the original though, I shouldn't think."

Pauline swallowed and chanced her luck.

"*Better*, I'd say."

That's it, Ally thought, stand up for yourself.

"*Better*?" Dad stopped by the door of his and Mum's room, still fumbling in his pockets for the keys. "Better than the *original*? Then I'll have to check it out for myself sometime. Oh yes I will." Then he punched the air and yelled "We are the champions!"

He found the key at last and opened up.

"Has he been drinking?" Ally asked her mum.

"He doesn't need to," her mum said. "If only it were that simple. If it was drinking that did it, he could give it up. But he can't. It's not drinking. It's *him!*"

"I," said Dad, "am just naturally cheerful. Except when I'm depressed. But even when I'm depressed, I'm still cheerful – for someone who's miserable." He held the door open invitingly. "Come in, ladies," he said, "and have a coke from the mini-bar. The refreshments are on me – seeing as it's your birthday, Ally, eh?"

Birthday. How irrelevant it seemed. What did birthdays have to do with it? It was only Stevie Manns that mattered.

But all the same, Ally and her mum and Pauline had to traipse in behind him. The room was virtually identical to the one next door. The only things different about it were the two paintings on the wall, and even those were so similar to the ones in Ally's and Pauline's room that they may as well have been the same.

Dad opened up the mini-bar.

"This is the life," he said. "A fridge in your bedroom. We should have this at home."

"You could always sleep in the kitchen, I suppose," Mum suggested. "That's almost the same thing. And the amount of time you spent with the fridge door open, wondering what to eat next, you practically live in it anyway."

"I was trying to keep a cool head," Dad said. "That was all." And he laughed like it was really hilarious.

"Cokes, is it?" he asked Ally and Pauline.

"Diet," they nodded.

"Diet," he said. "But of course. Sugar-free. Think of your figure."

"Think of your teeth," Ally said.

"Have you ever thought of thinking of *your* figure?" her mum asked him.

"You can't improve on perfection," her dad said, looking down at his waistline. He could easily have lost a stone and not missed it. "I fill these trousers a treat."

Pauline went and got a bucket of ice from the ice-maker in the corridor.

"And for your good self?" Dad asked Mum. "What will you have?"

"Orange juice," she said.

"As you please. And for me, I shall throw caution to the winds and have a small bottle of beer. It's madness, I know. But there you are. I don't care what people say. And besides, this is a special day." He handed the drinks around, then he raised his beer bottle.

"Use a glass," Mum said.

"Can't be bothered," he told her. "To Ally," he said. "Happy birthday."

"To Ally. Happy birthday," Mum and Pauline chorused.

They clunked bottles and glasses and sipped their drinks.

"So," Dad said. "What have you two been doing? Up on the roof, you say?"

"The roof? Why were you on the roof?" Mum asked, instantly worried about nothing.

Ally and Pauline shared a look. One that meant *don't say any more than you have to*.

"Oh, we went up to look at the roof garden, Mrs Morgan," Pauline said.

"Garden? On the roof?" Dad said. "How do they get the lawnmower up there?" And he laughed again, like he always did when he thought one of his jokes was specially funny.

"There isn't a lawn up there, Mr Morgan," Pauline

said solemnly, though Ally knew she was cracking up inside, "just plants in pots and stuff."

"Oh," he nodded. "Right." He took a sip of his beer. "Well Ally," he said, "me and your mum will be eating late at this dinner dance thing here. What are you two going to do for a meal?"

Food! How could he talk about *food* at a time like this. Ally felt too excited to eat a thing.

"I don't think I really want anything, Dad."

"Me neither," Pauline said.

Mum looked up from filling in the drinks list and said the usual.

"You have to eat *something.*"

"Yes, Mum," Ally sighed.

"That concert won't be over till gone ten. You'll be starving."

We won't, Mum, she thought. *We'll be living on air. Walking on sunshine and drinking fresh starlight. Stevie Manns, Charlie, Nitz and Bobby R — the complete nourishing diet with all the vitamins and minerals you could need. And all you have to do is listen to it. It's like a snap, crackle and pop that you never need to put a spoon into. The sound alone can keep you alive forever.*

"I know!" Dad said. "Why don't you both go down to the coffee shop and get something. Here."

He reached into his wallet and took out another note

– a tenner this time. It was money no object at all with him today.

Ally felt guilty at him spending all his money and didn't want to take it.

"Are you sure, Dad? You've paid for everything already, the concert tickets—"

"Your mum paid for them."

"Well, the hotel, the petrol—"

"Go on," he said. "It's your birthday. You two go down to the coffee shop and get something. By the time you've done that, it'll be time for you to get ready. Then I'll run you over to the concert hall in the car. Go on. Take the money. Give your mum and me a bit of peace for half an hour."

Mum looked up at him, but didn't say anything.

"All right. Thanks, Dad."

"Thanks, Mr Morgan."

"No problem."

He was at the window now, looking down into the hotel courtyard where legions of fans still stormed the building.

"I see my fans are still here," he said. "They almost mobbed me to death on my way in. Nearly had my trousers off."

"Dad!" Ally said, embarrassed. "Come on, Pauline. We'll go down to the coffee shop then."

"Okay, Ally."

"Right. See you shortly, girls – but not *too* shortly," Dad said. And he winked at her mum, who pointedly looked the other way.

Ally and Pauline went down to the coffee shop, but they couldn't eat. They ordered coffees and Danish pastries (even though Ally's mum had told them to get *something sensible* and Ally knew that Danish pastries certainly didn't fall into her mum's *something sensible* category). They let the coffees get cold and they nibbled at the pastries, and poked them about and reduced them to piles of crumbs. But they didn't really eat them.

Pauline looked up at the coffee shop clock.

"Two hours," she said, "and they'll be on."

Ally suddenly felt very nervous and sick. As though *she* was the one who had to go on stage and perform in front of thousands of screaming fans.

"Shall we go and get changed?" she said.

"Better had," Pauline agreed.

They left the coffee shop. Ally put thirty pence under the saucer of her coffee cup for the waitress to find. You were supposed to tip people in bars and cafes. She was sure she'd heard that, or seen it in a film.

They crossed the foyer and headed for the lift. Outside darkness was already falling. Some of the fans had gone – maybe to get ready for the night's concert themselves. Others just stood there, faces pressed to the windows, some of them looking cold, shivering a bit, all hoping for a glimpse of their idols.

"The Five Nine have probably already left the building," Ally said.

"Slipped out in the laundry van," Pauline said, knowingly.

They'd both read in the fanzines how these things were done.

"They'll be round there tuning up, and testing the sound," Ally said.

"Making sure everything's just right," Pauline told her. "Checking the acoustics and that."

"Adding the finishing touches."

It felt like you were one of the chosen few, one of the inner sanctum, when you knew these things. It was good to be on the inside. You seemed that bit closer. It wasn't quite a backstage pass and an invitation to the party after the show, but it was something to be in the know all the same.

"I wonder where Marlene is," Pauline said.

"Stuck in a traffic jam, let's hope," Ally replied.

On that note of hope and optimism, they went up in the lift.

A small sign hung from the door handle of fifteen-fourteen. *Do Not Disturb*, it read.

"Your mum and dad must be resting," Pauline observed. Ally nodded her agreement.

They went into fifteen-twelve, and began to get ready for the concert. Pauline had the bathroom first, then Ally. They dressed, put on make-up, got their hair right, checked their appearances, asked each other how they looked, and each said the other looked terrific.

But Ally didn't feel it. And even if she really *did* look terrific, there would probably be someone at the concert who looked even *more* terrific. Someone who would eclipse her finery, the way the sun eclipsed the moon. And Stevie Manns would see only that girl and not notice Ally at all.

No matter how tall you were, there was someone taller; no matter how rich, someone richer; no matter how pretty, someone prettier. And even if by some fluke, you were the best today, it didn't mean that you still would be tomorrow. It all changed like the seasons and flowed like the tide; things came and went, and some vanished forever.

"It's like the big fight, this," Ally said.

Pauline looked up from the dressing table where she was sitting, applying eyeliner.

"What do you mean?"

"This must be how boxers feel when they're in their dressing rooms getting ready for the big fight," Ally said. "Or condemned people in prison, who're going to be hanged in the morning. Or guillotined," she added. "Or going to get get a lethal injection. Or the electric chair."

192

"Why do you get electric chairs?" Pauline said, irrelevantly, "but never electric tables?"

"Or shot," Ally said. "That's it. It's like waiting to be shot."

"Shot?" Pauline said. "Why shot? You don't feel as if you're going to be shot, do you?" She turned back to the mirror. "I don't feel like that at all," she said. "This is the greatest evening of my life." She looked at Ally. "Thanks, Ally."

"What for?"

"Asking me."

"Thanks for coming," Ally said. "I don't think I could manage it on my own."

The odd thing was that despite her nerves, Ally did feel that it was the greatest evening of her life too. Yet she felt like a condemned woman in a prison cell as well. And those butterflies in her stomach had turned to eagles and their wings beat against her heart.

One hour to go. Only *one* hour to go.

One hour to go? My God, they'd be late. They'd miss it. Someone else would get their seats. They'd never let them in. They'd never— *Rat-tat-a-rat-tat. Rat-tat!*

It was Ally's dad knocking at the door.

"You ready?" he called. "Are you fit?"

"Yes, Dad. Coming. You ready, Pauly?"

. Pauline nodded.

"Ready as I'll ever be."

They had a final look each in the full-length mirror.

"Okay."

Okay. That was it. *Lead us to the ringside*, Ally thought, *and let battle commence.*

They were on a mission.

Ally pushed open the door.

"Well, well!" her dad said. "What a couple of stunners!"

They grinned, half-amused, half-embarrassed. It was nice of him to say it, but compliments from your dad, they weren't like *real* compliments. Not like compliments from the outside, compliments that *meant* something. Not like compliments from, well, Stevie Manns for one, or Charlie for another.

If Stevie Manns had said, "What a couple of stunners!" that would have meant something really huge. Compliments times ten. But then, Stevie would never have used words like that. Not "what a couple of stunners". That was parent-language; your dad talking.

Stevie would have been cool. Laid-back. Oblique.

"Hey. Hey, yeah. Really great. Yeah, I like your – yeah. Okay."

And that was all you needed. And one of Stevie's "Yeah, okays" was worth a thousand of your dad's "stunners", no matter how well intended.

But the real surprise was Dad.

"Mr Morgan!" Pauline was saying. "You look quite a stunner yourself."

He was all dressed up in an evening suit. Dark jacket, white ruffled shirt, cummerbund, black bow tie, patent shoes.

"Yeah, really smart, Dad," Ally grinned. "We might even let you drive us to the concert."

"Who could ask for more?" Dad said. He led the way to the lift, his car keys jangling in his hand.

"Is that suit for your dinner dance, Mr Morgan?" Pauline asked.

"It's either that or I'm helping out the waiters, Pauline."

"Yes, Mr Morgan."

Ally rolled her eyes to heaven. She did a lot of that when her dad was about.

The lift was approaching. You could see the yellow light, flashing up through the display of numbers.

"So what's Mum wearing, Dad?"

"Nothing, at this moment, as she's in the bath. But I'm hoping she won't be coming down for her dinner like that, with nothing on but her shower hat."

"Dad!"

The jokes! The jokes. You could stand it, if it wasn't for the jokes.

"Here we are, ladies." They got into the lift. "And going down."

They left the hotel and went out through the revolving door. The thousands of fans were now down to under a hundred.

"I think the band will have gone to the concert hall," Ally said to a girl who was hanging round by the door, under the watchful gaze of a grey uniformed porter, ready to eject her if she tried to come in.

Ally felt sorry for the girl, as it was getting cold now and she hadn't brought anything warm with her. She was dressed in jeans and a sleeveless T-shirt.

"I know. But I'll wait," the girl said. "I might see them when they come back."

"That won't be for hours, love," Ally's dad said.

"I don't mind."

"I doubt you'll see them to be honest," the porter chipped in. "They'll probably smuggle them in round the back."

"I'll wait anyway," the girl said. "I don't mind wait-ing."

"You'll catch your death of cold," Dad said.

"I don't mind. I'll wait. I'll be all right. Honestly. I'll be fine."

"Does your mum know you're here?"

The girl hesitated, then said.

"Yeah, course. She's coming to pick me up later."

"Well . . ."

"I'll be all right," the girl said. "Honest. I'll be all right. I won't be any trouble. I'll just stand here and wait. Maybe I'll see them."

"Okay, well, we'd better go," Dad said.

"Are you going to the concert?" the girl said. "Have you actually got tickets?"

Dad turned to the porter.

"Can't you let her wait inside?" he said. "She's perishing."

"If I let one in, they'll all want to come in," the porter said. Then he added, so as not to make himself seem too hard, "It's not me, it's the management. I'm just doing what I'm told."

The National Exhibition Centre was only a few miles from the hotel, but the traffic going there was heavy and slow-moving, snarled and congested, as thousands of cars – most, by the look of them, driven by parents with their children and a friend or two in the passenger seats – approached the building.

"Looks like the school run," Dad muttered to himself. But neither Ally or Pauline heard him. They were looking out of the window and growing anxious.

"We won't be late, will we Dad? We should have left earlier."

"We'll make it, don't worry."

"I hope they don't start without us."

"When did you ever hear of a pop concert that started on time?" her dad said cynically. "Keeping them waiting and whipping them up into a frenzy is half the job, isn't it?"

"Not with the Five Nine," Ally corrected him.

"They don't treat their fans that way," Pauline said.

"Don't they?" Dad said, the cynicism still in his voice.

"No!" Ally said firmly. "They don't!"

"Oh."

That put him in his place.

The car edged forward a few feet.

"They've got it all in Birmingham, really, haven't they?" Dad said. "When you think about it."

"Eh? What do you mean?" Ally said.

"I mean, they've got the Bull Ring, they've got Spaghetti Junction, and now –" and he gestured at the cars in front of them, "– they've got Traffic Jam."

"Yes, Dad," Ally said. "Very funny."

"You're not laughing," he pointed out.

"We tried," Ally said.

They edged forwards a bit further.

"Who's got the tickets then?" Dad said.

Ally and Pauline sat bolt upright.

"The tickets! Oh no! The tickets! Where are they! The tickets!"

"It's all right," Dad said, complacently patting his wallet. "I've got them."

"Oh, very good, Dad," Ally said. "You just nearly gave us both coronaries, that's all."

They got there with about twenty minutes to spare. Dad dropped them off and handed them the tickets.

"Ask that man what time it'll finish."

Ally went up to a security guard, then returned to the car.

"Half ten, he says."

"I'll be here. Right here," Dad said, "at twenty to eleven. Got that? Twenty to eleven. Right here. That'll give you ten minutes to get out."

"Okay, Dad."

"Thanks, Mr Morgan."

"Enjoy yourselves."

"Bye."

Then he was gone, and they were gone, engulfed in an ocean of people.

Ally's dad got back to the hotel to find her mum sitting by the mirror, wearing a beautiful black evening dress, which you'd think might look too solemn and mournful, but which made her look young and radiant. She was putting on a little make-up and a spray or two of that perfume, the one she had got for Christmas.

The door catch clicked. She looked round to see him admiring her.

"Well, well. Who's the beauty then? Or have I come to the wrong room?"

"Get on! Did you drop them off all right?" Ally's mum said.

"No problems. Now, are you ready?"

Ally and Pauline went with the tide. There was noise and commotion all around them. And a great buzz of excitement in the air.

"Tickets! tickets! Can I see your tickets?!"

"T-shirts, sweatshirts, souvenirs!"

"Your genuine photographs! Your genuine official signed photographs now. Your genuine photographs!"

"Don't buy anything out here," Pauline said. "It's all touts. None of it's official at all."

"No," said Ally. "I know. It was in the official fan club letter."

"You should always buy your things inside at the official fan club stall."

"And then you don't get ripped off."

"Your tickets, please! Your tickets," a man called. "No need to push. You'll all get in if you've got a ticket."

Then Pauline stopped dead in her tracks.

"Oh no, I don't believe it! Can you see who I see?"

Pauline pointed at two figures not far ahead of them in the queue. It was Marlene Forrester and Tracey Norris, both of them dressed up to the nines. Tickets for the show and backstage passes for after no doubt tightly gripped in their sweaty hands.

It made you sick. Twice, at least.

"They didn't get stuck in the traffic then?" Ally said, disappointed.

"No, more's the pity."

"Want to say hello to them?"

"Not much. You?"

"I don't think so. 'Goodbye' though, that would be a different matter."

"Come on, keep moving, we're nearly in."

And Pauline nudged her forwards.

"Would you sell me your ticket? Would you sell me your ticket? Will *anyone* sell me their ticket?"

A girl was walking up and down by the queue, practically in tears. She had some five pound notes fanned out in her hand, like a magician doing a card trick.

"Will anyone sell me their ticket? *Please!*"

No one would.

"Over here, love," a man called to her. He was big and fat, with oily hair. "You want a ticket?"

But one of the security guards moved towards him and he melted away into the crowd.

"Where did he go?" the girl with the money cried. "I wanted a ticket."

"They're forgeries, love," the security man said. "You won't get in on one of those. They're worthless. He'll just take your money and you won't get in anyway. Why don't you just go home and try and get tickets for another time."

"There might not *be* another time," the girl said. "This could be the last one *ever!*"

People in the queue turned and looked at her, shocked.

"What do you mean? Last one *ever?*"

"Bobby R might be leaving to go solo. Haven't you heard? It was in the papers."

"That's rubbish," someone said disparagingly.

"That's just gossip. No one believes *that.*"

"And anyway, what if he did? *Stevie* would still be there."

"The Five Nine is nothing without Bobby R. Bobby R *is* the Five Nine," the girl without a ticket said.

"Fat lot *you* know about it, stupid—"

The security guard intervened.

"All right, keep moving," he said. "Less of the controversy." He turned to the girl. "Put your money away, love, before you get it stolen. Just be sensible now and go home."

"No, I'll wait," the girl said. "I might get a ticket. Or at least I can hear them through the wall."

The security guard shrugged and walked away from her to supervise another part of the queue.

"Would you sell me your ticket? Would you sell me your ticket. I'll give you twice what you paid for it. *Please!* Will you sell me your ticket?"

Then they were in. In and heading for their seats.

They saw Marlene and Tracey in their row, further back. And Marlene and Tracey probably saw them. But they didn't acknowledge each other.

It was all irrelevant now.

Up on stage the instruments were set out. The keyboards, drum kit, all the rest. Hundreds of lights were suspended from a structure of scaffolding. There were two huge video screens, banks of speakers, computers, mixing equipment, synthesizers, everything.

Some roadies were up on the stage – and you'd think that *they* were the star attraction, from the way they were swanking about.

"One, two. One, two. One, two," one of them said into a microphone.

"Three!" a sarky voice from the crowd shouted, as if to help him out with his counting.

"Who's the support act?" Ally heard a girl in the row behind them ask her friend.

She and Pauline looked at each other. *Support act!* What a question. Amateurs! What was the girl *doing* there? Did she call herself a Five Nine fan? The Five Nine didn't *have* a support act. They did the whole set, the whole thing, themselves.

Anyway, who *could* support the Five Nine? Who could come before them? They'd never get a note of music out or a word in. No matter how good they were. People would be booing them off before they even started.

Support act, indeed!

And then it happened.

It happened so quickly and suddenly, you hardly knew it had happened at all. But the roadies were gone, and the lights were dimming, and there was a man up there on the stage. His face and his voice were vaguely familiar. He was one of those "personalities" from Top Of The Pops or some programme like that; a Radio One DJ or somebody, trying to act younger than he was. But he probably got a couple of grand and a backstage pass and an invitation to the party after, just the same.

"– and so with no further ado—"

No further ado? What was that about? *No further ado*, indeed.

"The group that needs no introduction—"

"*So get off and stop introducing them then!*" a voice yelled.

"The one, the one and only, the one and only for ever and for always – Stevie Manns, Charlie, Nitz Grey and Bobby R Scott – the terrific, the fantastic *Five Nine!*"

Then he cleared off, and good riddance. And there they *were!* Just appeared. Didn't even appear. Just *were there*. And the music was playing. And they were already singing, already dancing. Not that you could hear them. Not at first. All you could hear were the screams. Screams and screams and screams.

Then there was someone shouting "*Charlie, Charlie,*

Charlie!" so loudly it almost burst your eardrums. And Ally looked and saw that it was Pauline, and that tears were streaming down her face. And then there was another voice, even louder than hers, yelling *"Stevie, Stevie, Stevie I love you!"*

And that voice was even more familiar.

For Ally recognised it as her own.

12

GOOD EVENING, BIRMINGHAM!

Ally's mum and dad sat in the hotel dining room. There were plants in there the size of trees, set in pots as big as rain barrels.

"They're not plastic either," Ally's dad said, reaching up and feeling one of the leaves which overhung their table.

"Don't!" her mum hissed. "The waiter's coming."

"So?"

The waiter moved towards them, carrying a bottle of white wine and an ice bucket. He put the bucket down on a stand by the table and showed the wine label to Mr Morgan.

"Sir?" he said.

Ally's dad and mum exchanged a look. Then her dad said, "Seems fine." And he looked at her mum again. She knew and he knew that he had no idea whether it was fine or not. But they knew enough to know that it was what you were supposed to say – even if they hadn't eaten out much.

"Seems fine," you were supposed to say. And the next step was . . .

The waiter poured a trickle of wine out into Mr Morgan's glass and waited for him to taste it. He took a sip and rolled it around his mouth, as he had seen it done on the telly.

"Seems," he said after a lengthy pause, "fine."

So it was all fine. The label *and* the contents. Ally's mum was having a hard time stopping herself from giggling. The waiter filled her glass, then topped up Mr Morgan's glass, then put the bottle into the bucket of ice. He made a small bow and said, "Enjoy your meal, madame, monsieur," and he went.

They watched him go.

"Think he's really French?" Mum said.

"About as French as I am," Dad told her.

"Oh, *that* French."

"It's all swank," Dad said.

"It's all included though," Mum said, with a small smile. "I mean, the swank's all included in the price. You don't have to pay any extra for it."

"Are you taking the mickey out of me?" Dad said.

"Would I?" she asked him.

"Wouldn't you?" he said back.

"Anyway," Mum said, "I think he *was* French."

"You'll believe anything," Dad told her. "I wonder when the food will be coming. I'm starving."

He looked down at the great array of knives, forks and spoons which were arranged around his place setting.

"Enough tools here to build a battleship," he observed.

"Enough to eat a battleship," Mum said.

"Start from the outside and work your way in, don't you?"

"That's it," Mum said. "I think."

"Bread roll?" he asked, proffering the bread basket. She took one. He took two.

"Don't fill up on rolls," she said. "You won't eat your dinner and remember you're picking the girls up later – so don't drink any more of this wine."

"Hey," said Dad," when the kids aren't here, you start on me."

"You *are* a kid," she said.

"You like to think," he told her. "Mind you," he said, appraising her appearance, "You're not so ancient yourself."

"Thanks," she said.

"In fact you look pretty good to me."

"You don't look so bad yourself. You should wear a dinner suit more often."

"No, it wouldn't be a novelty then. Besides, if I went round in a suit like this, people would think I was a bouncer." He raised his glass in a toast. "To us!"

Mum raised hers. Their wine glasses clinked together.

"To us," she repeated.

"And to Ally," Dad said, "and to Cheryl. And to all the sleepless nights when they were babies."

"And all the others since," Mum added ruefully.

"To all the vegetables they wouldn't eat," Dad continued, "to all the rooms they wouldn't tidy up, to all the quarrelling they wouldn't stop, to . . ." he hesitated a moment, then added ". . . to how quiet it'll be when they leave home. If they ever *do* leave home."

A waitress approached with two plates on a tray.

"Here's the starters now," Dad said.

"They call it *hors d'oeuvres* on the menu," Mum informed him.

"They can call it what they want," Dad said. "It's still starters."

The waitress put the plates down, smiled, and left them to enjoy their meal.

"I think I'll have another bread roll with this," Dad said. "Pass them over."

"That's your third one," Mum told him. "Not that I'm counting."

"No, and anyway, it's all included," he reminded her.

"Yes," she said. "I thought it might be."

A man in a white dinner jacket entered the dining room. He crossed to the grand piano in the alcove, opened the lid, sat down on the piano stool, and began to play. He played, very softly, standard tunes from old Fred Astaire and Frank Sinatra films. And then he played

209

some Beatles numbers, but he made these sound as if they had come from Fred Astaire films as well.

"Nice to have a bit of music with your dinner," Mum said.

"If you can call it music," Dad said. "He sounds like he normally plays in a lift."

"In a lift?"

"He sounds like that piped music you get in lifts. You know, where they murder all the tunes and they all come out like sludge."

"I think it's very relaxing," Mum said, as the pianist trilled on the high notes at the right-hand end of the keyboard.

"Saves you buying sleeping pills, I suppose," Dad said. "I wonder how Cheryl's getting on at home," he added.

"I wonder how Ally's getting on at her concert," Mum said. "I hope she's enjoying it."

"STEVIE, STEVIE, STEVIE!!!"

A massed chorus of wailing voices shouted his name.

So he took his shirt off and the place went wild.

Not that he took it off just for effect. He needed to take it off. The band had only finished the third number, but he was already streaming with sweat. Both him and Charlie – for they were the ones who did most of the dancing. Bobby R wasn't really built for dancing, he was built more for writing songs, and obviously Nitz wasn't in much of a position to do any dancing, as it's a bit tricky to play the drums and dance at the same time.

"STEVIE STEVIE!!! TO ME!!! TO ME!!!"

He didn't aim it to anyone though, he just took it and hurled it into the crowd. A spotlight hit it, and the shirt looked for a moment like a great bird, a great albatross, winging across the auditorium.

"ME! ME!"

A thousand hands reached out for it. Three or four managed to seize it simultaneously.

"It's mine!"

"Mine!"

"I got it first!"

"Give it to me!"

Some kicking, punching and scratching followed as four girls quarrelled over the shirt. Two shaven-headed security men, dressed in the kind of suits that Ally's dad was presently sitting eating his dinner in, headed for the fracas.

"I wish he wouldn't do that," one said to the other. "Chuck his shirt in. It always causes trouble."

By the time they got to the trouble, it was over. The shirt had been torn into four segments and each girl was hugging a piece to herself. One was crying over her remnant.

"Stevie," she sobbed, "Stevie. I've got his arm. I've got Stevie's arm."

"GOOD EVENING BIRMINGHAM!"

The place went wild again.

It was Charlie taking the lead vocal this time. And taking *his* shirt off too.

"IT'S VERY HOT TONIGHT."

The place went even wilder.

"ARE YOU HOT?"

"YES!"

"I CAN'T HEAR YOU?"

"*YES!!!*"

"HOW HOT ARE YOU?"

"*HOT!*"

"ARE YOU HOT ENOUGH TO BOOGIE?!"

"*YES!!!*"

"ARE YOU HOT ENOUGH TO FUNK?!"

"YES, YES, *YES!!!*"

"ARE YOU TOO HOT TO COOL DOWN?"

"*YES!!!*"

And then they were into it. The first half dozen notes of the bass riff intro kicked it off, then the synthesizer came in, and then Nitz hit the snare drum. And then the horns joined in and the whole place erupted to the opening bars of *Too Hot To Cool Down*.

And some people said that the Five Nine were just a ballads band and couldn't hit a groove. Or said they were only a studio band and that Bobby R did it all with session men and samplers and smoke and mirrors. And some people said they couldn't even *sing!* Well! And that they couldn't *dance.* Well, seeing was believing. Hearing was believing. And seeing and hearing was – well, incredible.

"Sit down, sit down! No dancing on the seats there! Sit down!"

But no one noticed. The bouncers stalked the aisles giving orders which nobody could hear and to which they would have paid no attention anyway.

Ally was up on her feet. Pauline was up on hers. The band hit the chorus.

"*Too hot* (woa yeah) *to cool down* (that's right)
Too tired (who me?) *to wake up* (that's nice)
Too much (too much) *I'm in love with you baby*
Too hot, too tired, too much.
Pour water (cool water) *on my fire* (my fire)
Put your hand (cool hand) *on my brow* (that's how)
Too late (too late) *I just can't wait,*
I'm too hot to cool down now."

Then suddenly they cut the music. And there was Charlie singing the chorus again and just clapping his hands together to keep the rhythm. Then Stevie came in, singing really high, in falsetto, repeating the lines, about half a beat behind. Then Nitz left the drum set and came front stage to take a singing mike and he took the bass

213

line. And he was good, really good. He had this low, soulful voice that you never normally heard. Then Bobby R stepped forwards, leaving the keyboards, and he picked up a tambourine to add to the beat. He took the lead line together with Charlie and they went into the chorus again.

By this time the whole auditorium was clapping the rhythm, and thousands of voices were singing along. Stevie grabbed a hand mike and pointed it towards the audience, as if to say, "Here you are, it's *your* turn, it's *your* show. *You're* the stars now, and *we're* the audience. *You* sing for *us*."

And although you knew it wasn't true, though you knew it was just pretend and that they were the *real* stars, and you were just another face in the crowd, and no amount of saying otherwise made it any different, you still went along with it. You couldn't help yourself. It just carried you up, swept you along, got inside you like some sort of fever.

"Pour water (cool water) *on my fire* (my fire)
Put your hand (cool hand) *on my brow* (that's how)
Too late (too late) *make no mistake,*
I'm too hot to cool down now."

Then the band picked it up again. The four of them, arms round each other's shoulders, all singing into the same two mikes. And the crowd went wild. Absolutely totally, screamingly, bring-the-roof-down *wild!*

"Too late (too late) *it's at a melt-down state,*
I'm too hot to cool down now!"

Then the backing singers were with them. The three black girls and the two white girls who had been standing at different mikes at either side of the stage. They joined the band centre stage and shared the same microphones. Stevie put his arm around one of them to bring her in closer.

"Stevie, Stevie!" a broken hearted voice sobbed "do it to *me!*"

But he couldn't have heard a thing.

"Too hot to cool down now!"

The backing singers went back to their corners. Stevie picked up his guitar. The band took up the beat again and launched into the final chorus. The horn section joined in and took it on up to end on a blisteringly raw high note. Feedback blasted through the air; Nitz hit the drums in a great crescendo; and finally, it stopped.

They went wild. Absolutely, utterly *wild!* For four solid minutes you could hear nothing but the screams.

"THANK YOU! THANK YOU, BIRMINGHAM! YOU'RE A FANTASTIC AUDIENCE. THANK *YOU!*"

Ally heard herself screaming. *Was* it her? And who was that girl next to her? The one with the tears running down her face? The one who kept yelling, "*Charlie, Charlie, Charlie!*" all the time She did look familiar, and

215

yet was it someone she knew? Pauline, yes, it *was* Pauline. And yet, *did* she know Pauline? She'd never seen her like this. She seemed possessed.

"Charlie, Charlie, Charlie!"

And why was she screaming for Charlie? He looked quite ordinary to Ally. He looked all right, but nobody *that* special.

Stevie though, now he *was* special. Extra special. Special in an extra special way. And if you couldn't see how special he was, well, what did that make *you*, apart from one of the saddest people who had ever lived? So that was *your* loss, Bozo, if you couldn't see how special a person Stevie Manns was.

"OKAY, BIRMINGHAM!"

It was Bobby R at the microphone now. He looked off to his left and made a gesture at one of the technical back-up people.

"WE'D LIKE TO TAKE THE LIGHTS DOWN NOW—"

Down they went. Almost down to darkness. They glowed in warm reds and golds, creating – even in that vast hall – an atmosphere of intimacy. There was just you and them now. You and *him*. You and thousands of others, yes, but the thousands of others seemed no more than items of furniture in a room. Inanimate objects without pulses or souls. There was just you and the Five Nine alone.

"AND SLOW THE PACE DOWN WITH A LITTLE SONG WHICH YOU MIGHT KNOW—"

"*Tears Cry No More*, Bobby, *Tears Cry No More!*" a voice rang out.

"ONE WHICH HAS BEEN VERY GOOD TO US, AND WHICH WAS A BIG NUMBER ONE FOR US ALL AROUND THE WORLD—"

"Bobby! Bobby!"

"A SONG WHICH I AM VERY PROUD TO HAVE WRITTEN, BUT WHICH NOBODY CAN SING BETTER THAN . . . STEVIE! MR STEVIE MANNS!"

Bobby sat at the keyboard. Stevie took a breath.

"Two, three, *four!*"

And there you were, listening to the saddest and the most beautiful song ever. The most beautiful song ever sung.

"Tears cry no more
No more can I say
I loved you so much
But you went away

Now I'm alone
Alone at your door
Answer my prayer
Tears cry no more."

Throughout the darkened auditorium, small firefly lights began to go on. Pen-lights which people had brought with them, matches, cigarette lighters. The bouncers prowled the aisles again.

"Put that match out! Oi!"

No one paid any heed. The lights glistened and glimmered. The song was like a hymn, an anthem for a whole generation of people who didn't quite somehow fit in, or yet have a place in the world, and who maybe never would.

It was a song about loss and loneliness and love and being young. It described feelings that older people had surely long since forgotten. It was a song about love, *real* love. Not mum and dad kind of love, but true, intense, deep and forever, Romeo-and-Juliette, can't-live-with-out-you love.

And oddly, it was a sort of love you could feel even when you weren't actually *in* love with anyone. Because it was love for the whole world and all the people and things in it. It was about your whole life – what it had been, and what it would become.

As well as being sad, the song was full of hope too. Full of hope and strength, and a belief that it would all work out somehow. That even when your heart was broken and in pieces at your feet, even when you were all alone, and no one understood or cared, even though you lived in such a messed-up world with so many things wrong, with wars and pollution and cruelty – even then there would come a time when your tears would cry no more. And all your prayers would be answered. And the world would be beautiful again.

A drop landed on Ally's hand. She looked up, thinking for a moment that the roof was leaking. But, of course, it was only a tear. She wasn't the only one crying either. Many others were too. And many others were pretending not to cry, but crying just the same.

"One day," a voice inside her seemed to say, "it'll all work out. One day, we'll all be happy. And the world's tears will truly cry no more."

And then it ended.

Just when you wanted it to go on forever. The last chord echoed through the hall. There was silence. Like the silence in a church. Then before anyone could applaud, before you even got the chance to wipe your eyes, the lights were up, and the beat was thumping, and the band were straight into *No Time To Party* before you knew it. And the sadness was gone in an instant and the whole mood had changed, and everyone was back on their feet.

And then – and then – and then—

Then Nitz was at the microphone.

"THANK YOU BIRMINGHAM FOR A WONDERFUL EVENING! YOU'RE THE BEST BIRMINGHAM WE'VE EVER KNOWN!"

Trust him. Trust him to come out with something crazy like that.

"AND NOW, FOR OUR LAST NUMBER—"

Ally's mind reeled. What was he saying? *What* did he say? *Last number?* But that wasn't *fair!* They'd only been playing for twenty minutes! How *could* they? How *dare* they? How could they shortchange their fans like this? They'd come all this way, paid all this money, bought all the records, and now to treat them like *this!* Only playing for twenty minutes!

Then she looked at her watch.

Ten twenty-five.

Twenty-five past ten? Was that right? Then the band had been on stage for almost two and half hours. But that wasn't possible, was it? Where had the time gone?

"AN OLD ROCK AND ROLL NUMBER. ROLL OVER, BEETHOVEN!"

And they were away.

They played four encores and, if the fans had got their way, they would have played another four. (If the fans had really got their way, they would have played all night.) But after the fourth encore the lights came up and it was obvious that it was over. Ally felt both exhausted and exhilarated. She turned and looked at Pauline. Pauline's face was a mess of tears and ruined make-up, but she was smiling under it all.

"Do I look as bad as you?" Ally said.

"Worse," Pauline smiled.

220

They got out tissues and blew their noses and wiped their eyes.

"Fantastic, wasn't it?" Ally said.

"Fantastic," Pauline said. "Just – fantastic!"

They made their way towards the exit. It took forever. The crowd moved very slowly. In quiet corners members of the St John's Ambulance were consoling crying girls. One was on a stretcher weeping uncontrollably.

"But I love him," she wept, "I *love* him!"

"I know, love," the St. John's Ambulance lady said. "We *all* love him."

But this only made the girl worse.

"They don't" she said. "Not as much as *me!*"

They shuffled out past the official souvenir stalls, where the posters and the CDs and the photos and all the rest were on sale.

Ally bought a Stevie coffee mug as a souvenir and Pauline bought a set of Charlie pillow slips, so that she could sleep with her face next to his, she said. And she laughed a bit, as if it was silly. But it couldn't have been *that* silly, because plenty of other people were buying them as well. And they couldn't *all* be daft.

As they left the auditorium, Ally had the misfortune to see Marlene Forrester, the Professional Cow, and her sidekick, Tracey the Moo Moo, heading for a door marked STAFF ONLY. A bouncer at the door blocked their way, but Marlene held up her invitation and said, "We've got backstage passes. We won them in the fan club draw. They said to come here and someone would meet us."

The bouncer checked the invitation, found it to be authentic and said, "All right, this way. I'll take you round." He called to another security guard. "Watch this door would you?"

The other man nodded, and Marlene and Tracey followed the first man inside. As they went, Marlene happened to look back, and she caught sight of Ally and Pauline.

"Cooo eee!" she called. "You two! Did you enjoy the show? Great, wasn't it. Me and Tracey are going backstage now to meet the band. See you."

And the door closed behind her.

"I hope she drops dead," Ally muttered.

"I hope she suffers first though," Pauline added.

"I hope Tracey Norris drops dead as well," Ally said.

"I hope she suffers more."

"I hate them both. They're such big cows, they should be in milking parlours. Of all the injustice! That should be *us* going backstage. It's my birthday after all."

"We'd better go," Pauline said. "Your dad'll be waiting."

"Okay, I suppose."

He was waiting. Good old Dad. He did look like one of the bouncers in his dinner suit, and people kept coming up to him and asking him questions he couldn't answer, wanting directions and information about the Five Nine, and things like that.

He spotted Ally and Pauline before they saw him.

"You two! Over here!"

"Dad!"

"Hello, Mr Morgan!"

"How was it?"

"Oh, fantastic."

"Where's the car?"

"I had to park it. Come on."

"Where's Mum?"

"Waiting for me, back at the hotel. We're still dancing."

"Eh?"

"The dinner dance. At the hotel. Goes on till one. Come on."

They found the car and sat in the jammed traffic for twenty minutes, edging their way out. Ally and Pauline sat in silence, staring out into the night.

"You're not saying much," Ally's dad commented.

But what was there to say? If only they had got that backstage pass instead of Marlene and Tracey. If only.

"Well, I hope they're not going to keep us awake all night," Dad was saying.

His voice broke into Ally's thoughts. What *was* he on about now?

"Sorry, Dad? *Who* will keep us awake all night?"

"Your group," he said.

Pauline sat up and paid attention.

"How do you mean, Mr Morgan?"

"Their party, of course."

"What party?" Ally demanded.

"There's a sign in the hotel foyer, they put it up just as I was leaving to pick you up. Information, like. It says *Five Nine After – Show Party Guests, Please Go Up To The Penthouse Suite*. Well, that's just above us, the penthouse suite, so I hope they're not going to keep us awake all night, playing music and going mad."

Ally turned to look at Pauline. Pauline was with her, if not streets ahead.

The *party!* The after-show *party!* The Five Nine *after-show party!* It was at the hotel. The party was *right above them*. And true, they didn't have invitations, but maybe they didn't need them. Because parties could be gate-crashed after all.

At about the same time that Ally and Pauline returned to their Birmingham hotel, Cheryl arrived back at the family house along with her boyfriend Michael.

They sat outside in his car a moment. They had been to the cinema.

"Coming in for a coffee?" Cheryl asked.

"Could do," Michael said. "If it's not too late."

"No, no. It's only just gone eleven."

"How about your mum and dad?"

"No, they're not here, remember."

"Oh yeah. Well, if you're sure . . ."

"Only if you want to . . ."

"Well . . ."

Cheryl got out of the car and waited on the pavement as Michael went through his car security ritual. First he locked the steering wheel, then he set the car alarm, then he locked the car door, then he double checked that it *was* locked, then he looked up and down the street for any sign of suspicious characters likely to steal his vehicle. When he was confident that there were none, he followed Cheryl up the path, looking over his shoulder as he went.

She let them in to the house. Michael followed her through to the kitchen. She made some coffee and they took it through to the living room. Cheryl put some music on – one of Ally's Five Nine CDs, which was already in the player.

"I don't usually play this sort of stuff," Cheryl said. "Bit of a teenybop band, really."

"Yeah," Michael agreed. "Bit poppy. More for kids."

"Yeah," Cheryl said.

But neither of them made any movement to change the CD or to turn the music down.

The lush warm strains of *At Last We Are Alone* came

from the speakers. Stevie's voice was like cream: rich, sensual, smooth.

Michael took a sip of his coffee.

"Seems funny," he said, "your mum and dad not being here."

"Yes," said Cheryl, "doesn't it?"

She reached out and took his hand.

"Why don't you sit next to me," she said, "on the bean bag."

"You know," said Michael, "I think I might. It looks quite comfortable, that bean bag."

He joined her on it.

"Do you think my car will be all right out there, Cheryl?" he said.

"Yes," she told him. "I'm sure it will."

And after that, it was simple biology.

13

LET'S CIRCULATE!

There was still a handful of fans hanging around outside the hotel when Ally's dad drove into the car park. The others had gone home. The night had turned chilly and a light drizzle was falling. You had to be dedicated to stand out in the rain, risking colds, flu and pneumonia in the hope of glimpsing a distant figure, surrounded by bouncers, being rushed from a limousine to a door.

You probably had to be in love (or think you were) to do something like that.

It was after eleven o'clock when they entered the hotel, but the last thing either Ally or Pauline felt like doing was going to bed. It was partying all night they felt like. If only they could get invited to one – like one up on the penthouse floor. That would be just perfect.

"Come and see your mum," Ally's dad insisted. "Tell her about the concert." And he led the way into the dining room.

Several couples were dancing around the dance floor, in an old-fashioned way, doing what Ally's dad called "proper dancing". Though the way *he* did it, there wasn't much that was proper about it at all. It was more peculiar. Her dad was a bit of a two-left-feet job, and yet he generally managed to steer her mum around the floor without trampling on her toes too often.

"Have to be careful I don't tread on your mother," he'd say, "I can't afford the tights. Every time I ruin a pair, I have to buy her some. It's expensive, all this dancing."

Mum was sitting at their table, sipping what looked like a glass of—"

"Dad, is that *champagne?*" Ally said.

"No expense spared when I put my hand in my pocket," Dad said. "And I bought it myself, you know. It wasn't included. Do you want to try some?"

Ally looked at Pauline.

"All right," she said, and they each had a sip. Ally didn't like it all that much though, not as much as she liked the name. Champagne was yet another of those grown-up things which sounded better than it tasted.

Seeing their reactions, Ally's dad waved to a waiter who came over immediately. *Funny that*, Ally thought, *Dad getting the waiter to come over so quickly. You'd think they'd just ignore him.*

"Two Diet Cokes, please," he said, "for the young ladies."

And the waiter went off to get them.

"So how was it then?" Ally's mum said. "The concert?"

"It was —" Ally looked at Pauline "— fantastic."

"Fantastic," Pauline agreed, "completely fantastic." But she knew, and Ally knew, that there was no word, or combination of words, to really express *how* fantastic. You had to have felt it for yourself, you had to have *been* there.

"I remember when I saw the Beatles," Mum said. "I was even younger than you then. We all screamed so much, I lost my voice for three days after. Your gran got dead worried."

"And then your mum met me," Dad said, "and realised what a poor substitute George Harrison was for the real thing."

"Be quiet you," Mum said.

The Cokes arrived. Dad raised his champagne glass.

"Happy birthday, Ally," he said. "And many more of them."

"To the best one ever," Ally answered. "And thanks. For everything."

Ally's mum took a sip from her glass, then put it down.

"So what are you two doing now? Bed is it?" she said. "It is late."

"Ah, can't we stay up a bit?" Ally pleaded. "It is my birthday still. Can we stay up till midnight?"

Her mum and dad looked at each other.

"Can't see the harm in it," her father said. (Good old dad, everyone was innocent until proven guilty in his mind.) "It should be all right to wander about the hotel. It's quite safe."

"But not too late, mind," her mum said.

"Okay," Ally promised. "We'll maybe go to that coffee shop, eh, Pauline? I saw that it stays open till two in the morning."

"All right then."

They finished their cokes and went. As they left the dining room, the four piece band launched into *The Green Green Grass Of Home* and a dozen couples – Ally's mum and dad among them – took to the floor.

Ally looked at the four musicians as she left. They had Brylcreemed down hair – those of the band who still *had* hair – and though they couldn't have been that old (maybe in their thirties or forties) compared to the Five Nine, they might as well have been mediaeval. And the music could have come from the same era. It was hard to credit that such different sounds could be extracted from the same instruments. The way the Five Nine played their guitars, keyboards and drums, they set the place on fire. The way this lot played, they fizzled like a damp squib.

The name of the band was written on the front of the drummer's bass drum. The Hotel Hot Four it said.

Hot Four?

What was hot about them? They looked like they'd been embalmed.

Ally and Pauline left the dining room and headed – not for the late night coffee shop – but for the foyer of the hotel. They sat down on one of the leather sofas, feeling light-headed from the sip of champagne and the concert, and watched people come and go.

"I wonder when they'll all get here for the party," Ally said.

"They'll come in round the back, won't they?"

"I mean the guests, not the band."

"Why do you ask?"

"Just wondering."

"What?"

"If we could get in with them."

"Ally!" Pauline looked at her, rather shocked – or pretending to be. "Gatecrash the Five Nine party up on the top floor? How would we get in without invitations?"

"Pretend we're with someone," Ally said, surprised at her own boldness. "Just sort of tag along behind, get into the lift with them, blend in with the scenery, up to the penthouse with them, mingle with the mob, and then we're in!"

Pauline looked at her dubiously.

"It would never work . . . would it?"

"We could try."

"Right. Make-up repair first though," Pauline said. "I've just seen what I look like in that mirror. And you don't look much better. Have you seen your eyes? You look like a panda who's been to funeral."

They adjourned to the ladies cloakroom. It was quite a place. Big, grand and spacious, decked out in beautiful tiles.

"Look at all this *stuff*. Look at these mirrors. Look at these little towels. This toilet's bigger than our *house!*" Pauline said. "In fact it feels like a church in here!" She couldn't get over the place.

"Pauline, when do you get mirrors and towels in church?" Ally said.

"No, I mean, you just feel it would be all wrong to go to the toilet in here. It's so perfect."

"Well, perfect or not, I've got to go," Ally said, and she went off to one of the cubicles.

Pauline also opened a cubicle door, and peered inside.

"It's enormous! It's like a drive-in burger bar!" Ally heard her mutter, and then the door banged shut behind her.

They repaired their make-up in front of the mirrors, then wiped their hands on the deluxe paper towels (*Use Once And Leave In The Receptacle Provided*) and tried the free bottles of perfume.

They had a spray of everything and then, reeking of

232

expensive fragrances, left the cloakroom. A middle-aged woman in a lamé evening dress, carrying a jewelled bag, entered as they went out.

"Someone smells nice," she said, as she passed them. But then she started to cough.

They went back out to the foyer, trailing puffs of vapour like a couple of jets, and sat on a sofa by a pillar, which partially shielded them from the door. The guests for the Five Nine after-show party were starting to arrive. People they didn't recognise at first, then minor celebrities, people they'd seen on TV, that sort of thing. Most of them were clutching pale blue invitation cards, but others seemed confidently believing that their faces and reputations were their passports, and the only invitation they ever needed to get in anywhere.

They headed, loud and laughing, for the elevator to the penthouse. Some of them glanced around the hotel foyer as they went, holding their chins up to give themselves a good profile, maybe hoping that someone might recognise them, point them out, ask for their autographs even, or take their photos. Some were quite natural, but others had that *It's me, I'm famous!* look about them.

Ally turned to Pauline as a female children's TV presenter she didn't much like crossed the hall with her minor celebrity boyfriend in tow. He was supposed to be a comedian – not that Ally thought he was funny.

"No one important," she said to Pauline. "Just the C List."

Only she said it rather too loudly, for the woman turned and glared at her. Well, she could glare all she wanted, Ally thought, it was only the truth. It wasn't as if she was really someone. Not like Stevie, not like Charlie, not like Nitz and Bobby R. For who was *anybody* compared to them?

Besides, anyone could be a children's TV presenter. It wasn't exactly *difficult*, was it? All you had to do was grin a lot, and get excited about nothing and talk down to everyone as if they were mentally retarded. It was like being a DJ. It was the sort of job for people who needed attention and wanted to show off, but who weren't really all that good at anything.

The limousines began to pull up outside the hotel. A couple of photographers appeared and flash bulbs started going off.

"Paparazzi," Ally said.

"Who?" said Pauline.

"You know," Ally said, "gossip column photographers. Pictures for *Hello* magazine and stuff."

"Watch out," Pauline said. "Look out there. Do you see what I see?"

A large black limo with tinted windows had drawn up outside. And who was getting out of it? The President of the United States?

Not exactly.

It was Marlene Forrester and Tracey Norris. *Unbelievable!* Marlene Cow and Tracey Moo Moo in a car like that! A bus was more their style – a clapped-out one.

They were accompanied by a trendy looking woman in her late twenties, who was carrying a briefcase and who looked as if she had been born with a mobile phone in her hand.

"Must be in public relations," Ally said. "Must be from the fan club or the record company. Looking after them in case they get lost."

"Don't let them see us," Pauline said. "If I see Marlene Forrester smirking like the cat that got the cream, I won't be held responsible."

They hid behind the pillar as Marlene and Tracey and the woman in charge of them crossed the hall. The woman must have been delegated with the task of chaperoning Marlene and Tracey around and making sure they didn't get taken advantage of by lecherous roadies. She had got them to wear large name badges which said:

Official Five Nine Fan Club Visit Winner
Sponsored by
Big Hits Magazine.

"What an *embarrassment*," Ally hissed to Pauline. "Having to wear *that*."

"Bag-over-the-head job," Pauline said. "It takes the edge off it a bit, everyone knowing that you only got into the Five Nine party because you won the fan club raffle."

"Yeah, you look like a right charity case with a badge like that on," Ally said. "Like you're on a day out from an institution, and you've come up in the mini-bus."

They could see from the way that Marlene and Tracey were nervously fingering the badges, that they would have preferred not to be wearing them and that they would probably dump them, the first chance they got.

"Still, at least they're getting *in* though," Pauline said wistfully as the lift doors shushed to a close behind them. The orange indicator light rose in its column, going all the way up to P for penthouse, just under R for roof garden.

"It's not fair," Ally said. "What did *they* ever to do deserve it?"

Before Pauline could answer, a great raucous crowd of party-goers burst in through the front door of the hotel. Some of them looked like roadies, and some looked like members of the backing band, and Ally was certain that one of the girls had been one of the backing singers up on stage.

"Come on, Pauline," Ally whispered. "Now's our chance. Let's go."

"What? *Now*?" Pauline said uncertainly. She looked, and suddenly felt, very nervous.

"It's now or never."

"Now then. Right."

They stepped out from behind the pillar and mingled in with the party-goers. Conversation buzzed around them as the group made its way towards the lifts.

"We won't all get in one lift, will we?"

"Press the other button, will you?"

"Is there room for a small one?"

"Room for a fat one, you mean!"

"Ha, hah, ha!"

"Who are you calling—"

"Hello, hello—"

Ally turned her head. A man in dark glasses was looking down at her.

"Two more for the joy ride is it?" he said. And he held the lift door open so that she and Pauline could both squeeze in.

"Thanks," Ally said.

"Very kind," said Pauline.

"You're more than welcome. And up we go!"

He pressed the button and the lift ascended. Ally was relieved to see that none of the party-goers in the lift was carrying an invitation. And if they didn't have them, then she and Pauline probably wouldn't need them either.

They were *in*!

Or were they?

The lift stopped and the door opened. They were at the penthouse floor. Music was coming from somewhere nearby, along with the sound of laughter and talking. "And here we are!" the man in the dark glasses was saying. "Just follow your leader!" And he broke into a couple of bars of the Gary Glitter song as he led the way along the corridor.

"*I'm the leader, I'm the leader*
I'm the leader of the gang, I am!"

A woman in skin-tight jeans and a Lycra top which stopped just above her midriff, leaving her navel bare, took the man's arm and followed him in the direction of the music.

When they got to the door of the penthouse suite itself, a large bouncer (and they were *always* large) was stationed there, checking invitations.

"See your invite, please?" he said to the man in the sunglasses. The man reached into his coat pocket and took out a pale blue card.

Ally's heart sank. They all *did* have invitations after all.

"Danny Taylor and guest," the man said, and he handed his card over.

Danny Taylor? Ally knew that name. *He was a record producer, wasn't he? Didn't he have a credit on the first Five Nine album?*

"In you go, Dan," the bouncer said. "Sorry I didn't recognise you." Then he turned to Ally and Pauline.

"See your invitations ladies?" he said.

Ally made a pretence of looking for it in her bag.

"Oh, *no*, I've left it down in my coat, in the car. But we came up in the lift with Dan," she said. (As if Dan were an old friend from way back) "So if you can just let us—"

"Sorry," the bouncer said. "I've got to see it. I'll have to insist on seeing your invitation, I'm afraid. The orders are to keep security very tight."

"Oh, okay. We'll go back down and get it," Ally said. "Won't be a minute."

"Sorry."

"That's okay."

"Only doing my job."

"Don't worry," Ally said. "No problem."

So Ally and Pauline had to go back down to the foyer. As the lift door opened and they went to get out, they were confronted by another group of people, about to go up.

"Allo, 'allo, Leaving already?" someone said. "Can't be much of a party."

"We'll soon liven it up then," a woman said, and she cackled with laughter.

They got into the lift, their blue invitation cards in their hands, and up they went.

Ally and Pauline sat on the sofa in the foyer. The clock above the reception desk said that it was ten minutes past midnight. The tired night porter looked over at them.

"Did you want anything?" he said.

"No, we're fine, ta," Ally said.

"The coffee shop's still open if you want a snack," he reminded them.

"Thanks."

From the dining room they could hear the Hotel Hot Four playing *Save The Last Dance For Me*. It sounded like a dirge. It didn't sound like they were playing the tune at all. It sounded like they were cremating it.

"Best go to bed then, I suppose," Pauline said.

"I suppose," Ally said, bleakly forced to admit defeat. "And yet . . ."

And yet how *could* she give up now? How could she when Stevie was there? Up there, a few floors away, a few seconds' journey in the lift.

Just a minute!

"Pauline . . ."

"What?" she yawned.

She wasn't starting to flag, was she? Ally thought. *Pauline, don't let me down now.*

"One last try," Ally said. "What do you say?"

"Oh, all right then," Pauline said. "Why not?"

Atta girl! You are my best friend. You are a best friend among best friends, Pauly. You really are. You've heard of a musician's musician? Well, you are a best friend's best friend.

240

"So what do we do this time," Pauline asked, "to get up there? Do we put rubber suckers on our feet and climb up the front of the building?"

"Not quite. But we'll try that next if this doesn't work. Come on."

"Where are we going?"

"The back stairs of course," Ally said. "Where else?"

Ally led the way to the lift. They got in and she pressed the button for floor fifteen, their floor, the one below the penthouse. The lift went up.

"But the back stairs won't be any good, Ally," Pauline said. "There was a man in a monkey suit there this afternoon. Remember? We've already tried that."

"*That* was this afternoon," Ally said. "When there were thousands of fans outside. It's different now. It's quieter. Let's go and see."

They took the fire stairs from floor fifteen up to the penthouse level. The music and conversation from the party grew more audible as they went up. Then they were at the fire doors.

"Come on."

Ally pushed one of the swing doors open a fraction and peered in. No one there.

"Let's go."

They went inside. They were unmistakably in the service area of the penthouse, where the linen and sheets and towels and so on were kept.

"This way," Ally said.

Not that she really knew where she was going.

They headed down a narrow corridor, approaching the music. They came to another door, a single swing door this time, with a circular pane of glass set into it, like a ship's porthole.

"Down!"

They crouched down and crept to the door. Ally slowly raised herself and peeked out through the glass. She could see heads and faces. Talking heads, animated faces. There was cigarette smoke, the clatter of bottles and glasses, the buzz of conversation.

"Okay," she said to Pauline. "Let's do it! And remember – confidence is all!"

"Confidence is all," Pauline said. "Let's go, bro!"

Ally held her hand out. Pauline gave her five. Ally pushed the door open.

And they were in.

In! At last!

Heads turned to stare at them.

What were those two girls doing coming out of the service door?

Ally thought fast. She turned to Pauline and said loudly and indignantly, "I *told* you the loos weren't down there, stupid!"

Pauline cottoned on and played her part laudably.

"Well, I wasn't to know, was I? And stupid yourself!"

"You looking for the loo?" someone said. "Down there, second on the right."

"Thanks."

Pauline and Ally moved on through the crush – and it *was* crushed. Music was playing, but it wasn't Five Nine music. Ally had read that in one of the fanzines. The group gave express instructions that their music was not to be played at their parties.

They were off duty now after all.

"Hey, hey, hey! You found your invitation!"

What? Who?

Ally looked round. It was the man with the dark glasses, Danny Taylor, the one in the lift.

"Yes, thanks," she said. "Left it in the limo. Forget me head it if wasn't screwed on. In fact, I do sometimes. Always going about without me head on, me."

"Yeah, yeah, right on!" Danny Taylor said, and he laughed long and loudly. Ally looked at the bottle of beer in his hand and wondered how many he had drunk. She hadn't said anything *that* funny, after all.

Ah, drinks now! Yes, that was the thing. Get a drink in your hand and you wouldn't look like such a sore thumb.

"Where's the bar?" she asked Danny.

"Over there."

"Thanks. Come on, Pauly. Let's get some refreshments."

She and Pauline went to the bar and helped themselves to a couple of orange juices.

"I'm not having any more champagne," Ally said.

"Me neither," Pauline said. "I'm high enough."

"Penthouse high!" Ally said, and they grinned.

They'd made it, actually made it. There they were at the Five Nine after-show party.

Now all she had to do was to find Stevie.

Music and conversation pulsed around them. The place was jam-packed now with celebrities and minor celebrities and people who were probably big names in something or other, but whose faces you never usually saw – the back-room boffins of the music business.

But where was the Five Nine? Where were Stevie and Charlie and Nitz and Bobby R? It was *their* party after all. So where *were* they? They must have returned from the concert by now? Hadn't they come to their own party? They must have done.

"Let's circulate," Ally said.

"Right," Pauline agreed.

They drifted on from room to room. The penthouse suite was vast and luxurious. It must have cost thousands of pounds a night to stay there. There were rooms leading off into other rooms. Bouncers guarded some of them. Maybe that was where the band was, in with a few favoured friends, unwinding and letting their hair down. Rooms within rooms and parties within parties. Maybe that was how it worked, all in layers, like an onion.

Perhaps gatecrashing the main party was just the beginning. Maybe they now had to gatecrash others, until finally they managed to penetrate to the ultimate party, where they would find Stevie and Charlie (and Nitz and Bobby R too, though frankly, they didn't matter so much).

They wandered on, with no one to talk to but each other, hearing snatches of conversation around them.

"Yes, I'm in A and R actually. And what do you do?"

What the hell was A and R?

Ally was dreading that someone would come up and put the question to her.

"And what do you do?"

"Me?" she'd have to stammer, "Well, I'm a schoolgirl, actually, I do reading, writing and 'rithmetic. And yourself?"

She'd be straight out on her ear then. Her feet wouldn't even touch the shagpile.

"Listen, if anyone asks," Ally said to Pauline, "we're in marketing."

"*Marketing?*" Pauline exclaimed. "What are we doing in marketing? Not only do I not know what it is, it sounds dead boring as well."

"Marketing," Ally insisted. "And distribution. That's what we've got to say. That should soon shut them up.

Marketing and distribution should pretty soon shut anyone up."

"Oh, hello!"

God, *no!* It was the bouncer. The one who had asked for their invitation earlier on.

"You found your invitation then?" he said.

"Yeah, yeah," Ally mumbled, "we gave it to −" she saw another dinner jacketed bouncer moving through the crowd "− to your mate."

"Rollo?"

"Yeah, is that his name? Yeah, Rollo, yeah."

"Oh, right. Well, enjoy yourselves."

"Thanks."

They hurriedly moved on.

"I think we're the youngest here, Pauline," Ally said.

"We are, definitely. And look at *them*. What are *they* doing here?"

A middle-aged, very ordinary looking couple appeared, coming out of the lift. The bouncer didn't even ask them for their invitation.

"Mr and Mrs Scott, wonderful to see you," he said. "This way."

"It's Bobby R's mum and dad," Ally said.

"Then they *must* be here. The band must be here. They *must!*"

"Watch."

They watched as the bouncer led Bobby R's parents

down along the corridor to where a velvet rope, suspended between two brass posts, sealed off further access. He unhooked the rope and led them through.

"They're down *there*," Ally whispered. "That's where the band is. They must all be down there. Oh Pauline . . . Stevie's there!"

"And Charlie."

"Stevie and Charlie! They're there. They're *there!*"

Before she could gather her thoughts, Ally suddenly heard a very familiar and extremely unwelcome voice in her ear.

"Ally Morgan! And Pauline Moore! What are *you* doing here?"

(Like *Look what the cat's dragged in.*)

And when she looked round, it was straight into the malevolent gaze of Marlene Forrester.

"How did *you* get in here?!" Marlene demanded, as though she owned the place or something and was about to blow the whistle on the wrong-doers.

"Well how did *you*, come to that?" Ally said back.

"*We*," Marlene Forrester said, preening herself until all her feathers stuck up, "won the fan club competition, didn't we? We *told* you that!" (*Yeah, and rubbed our noses in it*, Ally thought.) "So we're *entitled* to be here! But *you*'re not. So what *are* you doing here?"

("Winging it," Ally almost said. But she didn't.)

247

"Yes," said Tracey (The Side Kick) Norris. "How *did* you two get in? Who let *you* past the door! I bet you must have gatecrashed! I've a good mind to get you thrown out – on your ear."

"As a matter of fact," Ally said, preening herself every bit as much as Marlene, "*we* are staying in the hotel, aren't we Pauly?"

"Yes," Pauline said, "very much so. Beautiful room too. Got a mini-bar. And you should see the downstairs toilets!"

"Yes, and *we*," Ally continued, working up to the big fib, "got talking to someone."

"Danny Taylor!" Pauline said helpfully.

"The record producer!"

"*Big name* record producer," Pauline said, gilding the lily for all it was worth.

"And he said," Ally went on, " 'Why don't you come up and join the party. As my guests. As members of my star-studded entourage.' Didn't he, Pauly?"

"Yes," she confirmed. "He did. And so we accepted his kind invitation."

"And here we are."

"In person."

"So there you go."

"Stick that in your pipe and smoke it!"

"Yeah! So if *you're* not careful," Ally warned Marlene, "we'll have *you* chucked out – on your bum!"

"Exactly!" Pauline said. "So don't get fresh with us."

"Because we," said Ally, "are in with the in crowd!"

She felt there was no more to be said then, and that the enemy had been well and truly trounced. She and Pauline made to move off. But Marlene wasn't prepared to leave the one upmanship at that.

"Well *we*," she said, "saw the concert."

"Well so did *we*," said Ally, "didn't we? That's why we came here, stupid."

"Well *we* – stupid yourself," Marlene said, "got to go backstage after. And met absolutely *everyone*. Didn't we, Tracey?"

This was truly a blow. And Ally just had to ask.

"Did you . . . meet Stevie?"

Marlene looked at Tracey. And no matter what her words might now say, that glance had told the truth. They *hadn't* seen him. They had *not!* At least not yet anyway.

Ally felt that it was almost a victory.

"No we didn't quite meet the band, not yet," Tracey admitted. "But we're going to, any minute."

"There was a mix up, a misunderstanding. The band had already gone when we got there. But Fran –" Marlene pointed at their chaperone, the woman with the mobile phone, who was talking to someone across the room, "– is going to arrange it all now."

Ally's victory turned to defeat.

"So you're going to see them?"

"Any minute," Marlene smirked.

"Come on, Pauline," Ally said. "Let's circulate."

And she hurried away.

They left the smug and smirking Marlene and Tracey and went to the bar for more orange juice. It was hot now and Ally felt as if she needed something.

They took their drinks and wandered back across the room in time to see Marlene and Tracey in conversation with Fran.

"Get nearer," Ally said. "What's she saying?"

They edged close enough to overhear.

"And Stevie's really sorry," Fran was saying, "but he doesn't feel all that well, and Charlie's otherwise engaged, just at this moment, but Bobby R and Nitz say they'd be really pleased to say hello. So if you'd like to come through . . ."

Marlene and Tracey followed Fran along the corridor to where the velvet rope sealed off the private party.

Their faces were pictures of bemusement. They were going to meet Bobby R and Nitz, and that was incredible. Yet they were really, at heart, Stevie and Charlie fans, and they wouldn't be seeing *them*. So they had won and yet lost too. Failed and succeeded, and their triumph was tinged with disappointment.

Sweet and sour, Ally thought. *Like a Chinese meal. Like life.*

She and Pauline watched them go, as they vanished into the inner sanctum. It was as if they had gone to heaven and left ordinary mortals behind in purgatory.

"Did you hear that?" Ally said. "That woman said Stevie's not feeling very well. Or do you think that was just an excuse?"

"And where's Charlie?" Pauline asked. "She said he was 'otherwise engaged'. What does *that* mean?"

"I do hope Stevie's all right," Ally said, concerned.

"I wonder what Charlie's doing?"

Many painful possibilities crossed Pauline's mind of just what Charlie could be doing at a party which had rendered him "otherwise engaged".

Like biology.

Ally looked down the corridor towards the velvet rope which separated off the private party. The bouncer who had been standing there had gone. Maybe he had wandered off for a second to get himself a cold drink.

"Look," Ally said. "Pauline, *look!*"

She looked and saw and understood at once.

"We've got this far," Ally said. "It's probably our only chance. The only chance we'll ever have in our whole lives."

"Come on then," Pauline said. "Let's go!"

She walked swiftly down the corridor, Ally keeping up with her, step for step. They ducked under the velvet rope, pushed open the door in front of them, and there they were.

Somewhere.

Maybe in heaven.

And they hadn't even died.

14

DIED AND GONE TO HEAVEN

Clutching their drinks, they left the corridor and edged into a large room. Although not as crowded as the rooms on the other side of the velvet barrier, there was still quite a party underway. The lighting was dim, but several people were wearing dark glasses and – as they couldn't all be suffering from conjunctivitis – Ally assumed that they were just too cool for words.

Right at that moment, she wouldn't have minded a pair of dark glasses to hide behind herself.

"Now what do we do?" Pauline hissed at her as they sidled into the room.

"Play it by ear," Ally said.

"I can't. I'm tone deaf."

"We'll have to mingle," Ally instructed.

"I don't know anyone to mingle *with*," Pauline pointed out.

"Mingle anyway."

"Right, I'll mingle with you."

They saw Bobby R then, standing in a far corner of the

room, in conversation with a man wearing an Arman'
suit and a black T-shirt.

"Bobby," Pauline gasped. "Bobby R! In the flesh."

And funnily enough, there wasn't quite as much of
that as you would have thought. Close to, Bobby R was a
much slighter figure than he appeared on stage. Smaller,
more slender, quite (as Ally had been half-afraid)
ordinary really.

Pauline was thinking the same thing.

"He looks pretty ordinary, really. Doesn't he?"

Someone in dark glasses overheard, turned, looked at
Pauline, and gave a wry smile.

"Shh!" Ally said. "Don't embarrass us!"

You didn't make remarks like that in here. They were
all too cool.

Too cool for words.

Bobby R's girlfriend – Janey Mansell, one of the
backing singers – stood next to him, a drink in her
hand, as Bobby and the man in the Armani suit continued their conversation. She put her hand up to her
mouth to stifle a yawn and then she looked around the
room as if for someone else to talk to.

Bored. Yes, that was it, she looked *bored*. There she
was, right slap bang next to Bobby R, the greatest
songwriter in the world, who must be full of the most
interesting things to say and the most fascinating tunes
to whistle, and she looked utterly – *bored!*

"Who's the suit?" Pauline said. "The man that Bobby R's talking to?"

"Dave Marks, their manager, isn't it?" Ally replied. "His photo was in the magazine."

"Oh yeah," Pauline remembered, "of course."

A man in a leather jacket, who seemed to be at the party on his own, homed in on them.

"Allo, 'allo, and who 'ave we 'ere then?" he said. "Wot do you two do about the place?"

"We're schoolgirls, actually," Ally felt like saying, *"and we've gatecrashed the party. And who are you? And what do you think you look like in that stupid jacket?"*

But what she said instead was:

"Ally Morgan and Pauline Moore. P.R. I *do* hope you're enjoying the party. Any complaints, you let us know, and we'll try and put it right."

"Em – oh – yeah – great – fine –" the man stumbled.

"Well, *so* nice to meet you," Ally oozed, with all the sincerity she could muster. "*Do* enjoy yourself. And *do* help yourself to another drink and a few nibbles."

"Oh, right, yeah, ta," the man said.

"If you'll excuse us then . . ." Ally said. She gave the man a dazzling PR smile and turned to Pauline. "Come on Pauline, let's mingle, shall we, make sure everyone else is enjoying themselves?"

"Eh? Oh yeah, right, sure. Let's do that," Pauline said.

They moved on into the room, leaving the man behind.

"I thought we were in marketing and distribution," Pauline said. "What are we doing in PR?"

"Last minute change of plan," Ally said.

"What's PR anyway?

"You know, Public Relations."

"We'll be in BT in a minute, never mind PR," Pauline scowled.

"What? British Telecom?"

"No. Big Trouble," she said.

"Look," said Ally. "It's Nitz."

Nitz, the drummer, was – like Bobby – also standing talking to a man in a suit. He had his arms folded so that the tattoos on them were clearly visible. He was staring at the man with an expression of disdain, of dislike even. The man looked like a record company executive.

"And then what I thought we could do –" the man began to say.

But "No, I don't think so, actually," Nitz said, "I don't think so at all."

And he turned his back on the man and walked off to get a drink.

They spotted Fran then, the chaperone with the mobile phone. She was ushering Marlene Forrester and Tracey Norris over to be introduced to Bobby R. Marlene and Tracey stood like a couple of simpering yokels on the periphery of Bobby R's private circle, waiting for him to finish his conversation and to notice them.

Dave Marks, the man Bobby was talking to, turned and saw them all waiting.

"Fran. How are you?" he said.

"Can I interrupt you and Bobby a minute to introduce our competition winners?"

"Certainly. Please."

It was like being presented to royalty.

"Bobby, this is Marlene and this is Tracey."

"No, I'm Tracey, actually. She's Marlene."

"Sorry. Tracey and Marlene."

"Hi," Bobby said, "great to see you."

"Hi," Tracey said. "Great to see *you*."

They almost curtseyed.

Pauline and Ally watched from a discreet distance, half-hidden behind a big, fat man who was wolfing down the nibbles.

"Look at them," Ally said. "They've gone like jelly babies."

And it was true. Marlene and Tracey had turned to jelly. Their minds had gone blank. They could think of nothing to say to Bobby at all, other than, "We're your biggest fans."

"We *love* your songs."

"They're really good."

"Fantastic."

And though Bobby R did his best to make some kind of conversation with them, and to put them at their ease, they were too overcome by the majesty of the occasion to talk much sense or to say anything even remotely interesting.

"It's like they just met the Pope and got his blessing," Ally whispered, and Pauline began to giggle. Ally wondered in her heart though, how *she* would be if Stevie suddenly appeared. She wouldn't just be a wobbling jelly, she'd probably completely dissolve.

The strain of the one-sided conversation was obviously telling on Bobby R, so Fran wheeled Marlene and Tracey away to be introduced to Nitz. This encounter seemed to fare a bit better, and he soon had them both laughing at something he'd said. But it was an equally brief meeting, and soon the socially adept Fran was steering Marlene and Tracey away to meet lesser members of the entourage, obviously planning to have them out of the room within five minutes.

"Well?" Pauline asked. "Now what?"

Ally was reminded of what her mum had once said, about the barking dog chasing the car.

"But when the car stops, what does it *do*?" she had said. "What does it *do* with it? It doesn't have a clue, does it? And that's what all these screaming girls are like with pop groups. They scream that they want them, that

258

they'll die without them, but if they ever got them, what would they *do*?"

The only thing was, Ally hadn't quite caught up with her car yet. But if she did . . . well, she'd just have to see then.

"Well?" Pauline repeated. "Now what?"

"Go for broke, I suppose," Ally said.

"What does that mean?"

"Well, Stevie and Charlie are here *somewhere*, aren't they?"

"I suppose. And so?"

"So let's go and find them. We'll split up."

"What if anything happens?"

"The worst they can do is ask us to leave."

"See you back in our room then, if anything goes wrong. Fifteen-twelve?"

"Right. See you back in the room."

"Good luck."

"G'luck. And take no prisoners."

Ally wandered away. She slipped back out into the corridor and followed it along. There were rooms on either side, in darkness, or with their doors closed. She was nervous at the thought of just opening them, but then, if challenged, she could always say she was looking for the loo.

She pushed the first one open. Darkness. She found a light switch and put it on. It *was* the loo.

She turned that light off, closed the door, and went on down the corridor. She saw the glow of another light at the far end, where the corridor turned to the right. She seemed to hear the sound of voices too. A girl's voice at first – she was doing most of the talking – and then a boy's.

"I don't see why," he was saying, "I don't understand . . ."

Ally *knew* that voice. She knew it from a hundred songs played a thousand times over. She knew it in her dreams. It was Stevie – Stevie's voice. He was there – *there!*

She walked on towards the voices, treading as lightly as she could. She got to the end of the corridor and saw that the light was coming from a kitchen. (*That was good*, she thought, *a kitchen. She could say that she was looking for a glass of water.*)

She peered into the room through the crack between the door and the door frame. Two people were in there, Stevie and a girl. It was Caslile, the model. Ally almost gasped out loud. Not at the surprise of seeing her there – she was Stevie's girlfriend after all – but at the surprise of seeing how beautiful she was.

It was funny – because you read in these magazines, and people often said about models and actresses and people like that – that although they got on well with the camera, quite often in the flesh they were nothing much to look at. But that certainly wasn't true of Caslile. She was stunning. A great natural beauty, with a wonderful figure.

Ally suddenly felt immensely awkward, lumpy and gawky. She wished she hadn't come. She wished she hadn't gatecrashed the party. She wished she'd never even gone to the concert. She was just fooling herself. Who was she kidding? As if Stevie would ever—

But *wait! What* was that? What were they saying?

She stood and listened intently.

She had meant to tiptoe away, to go back, to find Pauline and just return to their room. But she couldn't. She couldn't move her feet.

They were having a row!

"But I don't see why . . . I don't understand. I just don't understand!" Stevie said.

No, it wasn't a row, it was something else. Emotions were high, but it wasn't a row. So what was it? What was going on?

"I'm sorry, Stevie, but it's how I feel. I'm sorry, really sorry . . . but that's how it is. I didn't choose for this to happen. It just did."

And then Ally understood. The realisation came over her like a great wave of heat.

My God! *My God!*

It was Caslile, she was dumping him. She was saying goodbye. To *Stevie Manns*. To *Stevie*, the most adorable, beautiful person in the world. Stevie, who could have had anyone, *anyone* he wanted!

And she was *dumping* him. Just like that.

Anger replaced the fire. How *could* she? How *dare* she!

"How *dare* you treat my Stevie like that?!" Ally almost screamed. But she stayed where she was, rooted to the spot, and didn't utter a word.

Because why would she want to scream a thing like that? That made no sense either. She wanted Stevie to be free, didn't she? To be free of Caslile and everyone else. Then he could be hers, *hers* alone. And everything that Caslile wouldn't or couldn't give, all the things he wanted and needed, Ally would give them to him. She would, without question. Ally would dry his tears and tell him that it was all going to be all right, and she would whisper that she loved him.

Just like in the songs.

Only it wasn't like in the songs, or in the films, or like it should be at all. People had forgotten their lines and their places and what they were supposed to feel.

They weren't carrying on like you did in the songs. This wasn't hurt and pain turned into music and lyrics, soft and cushioning and always one step removed. No, they were carrying on like you did in life.

When it was raw, and it hurt.

"But, Cass . . . Caslile . . . Cassy . . . I *love* you. I love you."

It was like the end of the world. Ally stood, her heart pounding, looking in through the crack in the door, spying on them, quite unashamedly, unable to tear herself away.

"I love you, Cassy. I *love* you."

He loved her! Ally's head swam. But *wait* a minute. Hold *on* now. That was just songs, wasn't it, just in the songs? I mean, Stevie *sang* about it, yes, sure, but that was a song. And Caslile, she was gorgeous and beautiful and all that, but surely they were just going out together. They were *people like that*. Yes, that's who they were. *People like that.* People who appeared in *Hello* magazine and in the *Mirror* on the pops page. *People like that.* And that's what they were, that was what you called them. And it was always different for *people like that*. It was all show and gloss and superficial.

I mean, people like that didn't *feel* like that, they didn't really mean it, did they? It wasn't for *real?*

But maybe it was. And maybe they did. Maybe despite being so rich and beautiful and famous and all the rest, they were just the same and hurt just as much inside.

And oddly, Ally had never thought of Stevie like that. That he was only human, only a human being like her, who bled when he was cut, and laughed when he was happy, and cried when he was hurt.

"I'm sorry, Stevie. I *do* like you, and it *was* good, for

263

such a long time, and it's so awful that it should be him—"

"No, that's okay, okay—"

"I'm sure we can still be friends—"

"Yeah, right, maybe . . . I don't know . . ."

"It's maybe best if I go now . . ."

He didn't reply. Ally couldn't see his face. He had his back to her. But he moved his hand up to his eyes in the kind of gesture you would make if you were wiping tears away, smearing them off, so that people wouldn't know you had been crying.

"Bye, Stevie . . . bye."

Caslile went to kiss him, but he didn't respond. She reached out to touch him, but then let her hand fall back to her side.

"Bye." Her voice was just a whisper. She turned and left the room.

Ally quickly ducked back around the alcove. Caslile came out of the kitchen and made her way along the corridor to where the party was still in progress.

What had she dumped him for? Ally wondered. *Who* had she dumped him for? Who could you possibly dump Stevie Manns for? Surely there wasn't anyone in the world.

She came out from the alcove and peeked back into the kitchen. Stevie had gone to the sink to get a glass of water. He sat down at the kitchen table. Took a sip from the glass. Sat motionless for what seemed like ages, staring at nothing, then he rested his head on his arms.

At first Ally thought he had fallen asleep. But then she saw that his shoulders were shaking, and then she realised that he was weeping.

She didn't know what to do. It was like a terrible accident had happened and they shouted "Is there a doctor in the house?" but there wasn't. And it was all down to you to do something, but you didn't know what, as you hadn't had the training, and the only thing you were really qualified to do was to panic.

It was like watching an animal suffer. But what made it worse was that she knew that she shouldn't be there, she shouldn't be watching him. He thought he was alone. Ally knew enough to realise that people who have been hurt have the right to cry and not to be seen by others. They have the right to their privacy, to be left to themselves to give expression to their feelings, until they feel ready to face the world again.

She shouldn't be there. She didn't *want* to be there, not now. Only she *was* there. Another human being was in anguish and distress just a few feet away from her and someone had to help them, to make the pain go away.

And there was only her there to do it.

She took a breath. She swallowed. She smoothed her dress and tried to tidy her hair. She went in.

"Stevie . . ." her hand reached out and touched him

on the shoulder. (Yes, touched him, actually *touched* him, actually touched the shoulder belonging to Stevie Manns.)

"Stevie, can I help? Are you all right?"

He looked up. His eyes were red. He rubbed the tears away with his hands. Ally noticed a roll of kitchen towel by the sink. She tore a piece off and gave it to him.

"Thanks," he said. And he blew his nose. He looked sort of . . . sweet.

And confused.

"You don't have to say anything, Stevie," Ally said. "Because I understand."

"I'm sorry?" He looked bewildered.

"I understand."

"Oh. Understand what?"

She could hardly say she'd been standing there listening.

"How you feel," she said.

He looked at her.

"How can you know how I feel?" he asked.

She could have told him the truth.

"Because I love you, Stevie," she could have said, *"and I always have. Ever since I first heard your voice on the radio and ever since I bought your first CD. I've thought about you almost every waking minute since and I've dreamt about you in my every dream. I've loved you more than I ever thought you could love anyone. Loved you so much I could*

266

hardly do my homework. Loved you so much that all I ever
wanted was to be with you forever and ever and—"

And now here she was with him, and she knew – even
in her very attainment of the impossible dream – that
anything more would never be possible.

He was everything she had thought, everything and
more. More because she had seen him cry, and he had
revealed a sensitivity that she had known all along was
there. He *was* everything she had hoped. He wasn't a let-
down, he wasn't a phoney, he wasn't a sham. He wasn't
one person up on stage and another in private. He was
genuine and real and good and kind.

But Ally knew it would never be.

I'm just a schoolgirl, she thought, *with a crush on a pop*
star. That's what they'll say. No one will ever believe it's
more than that. They don't know. They'll never know. Not
that what they think matters. No, what's wrong is—

"How can you know how I feel?" Stevie repeated,
breaking into her thoughts.

"Because," Ally said, "I've been in love too."

Stevie looked at her.

"And did it work out?" he said.

"No," she said. "Not really."

"Why not?" he asked.

"Because," Ally said, "he wasn't in love with me. And
never would be."

"How did you know?"

"Oh, you know. You just know. You see, all because you love someone, it doesn't mean that they'll love you. No matter how much you might want them to. And the funny thing was, I never thought about that side of it. I thought, just because I love him, he'll love me, the moment he sees me, automatically. But life's not like that is it?"

"No," Stevie said. "I'm afraid it's not."

"It's what you learn," said Ally, "when you grow up."

"Yes," Stevie smiled. "Maybe. One of the things, anyway."

"But, you know," Ally said, "it was wonderful while it lasted. It was such a wonderful dream. It was the most wonderful thing in the world."

Stevie took a sip from the glass of water. He looked into her eyes. She looked away, embarrassed, then looked back. His eyes *were* blue. As blue as the sea.

"Were you listening at the door just then?" he said.

"Yes," Ally admitted.

"Sit down," Stevie said. He pushed a chair over in her direction with his foot. "What's your name?" he asked.

"Ally," she said. "Alice Morgan."

"Who brought you?"

"Nobody. I gatecrashed with my friend."

Stevie grinned at her.

"You *gatecrashed*? You got past all the security!"

"Yes. To see you."

"To see *me?*" He laughed. He seemed genuinely surprised that anyone would go to all that trouble, just to see him. "Well," he said, "you could have picked a better moment. You didn't exactly catch me at my best."

"You know," Ally said – and it took all her courage to say it, as it's not always easy to speak the truth – "I think that maybe I did."

And then there she was, there she *actually* was. Actually sitting there talking to Stevie Manns, just sitting there having at chat with him, just like he was *anyone*, just like he was really ordinary.

They must have sat there a good fifteen or twenty minutes just chatting about everyday things, about how the concert had gone, and what she thought of it, and what Stevie thought of it.

Stevie asked if there were any ways in which she thought the stage show could be improved. At first she said no, but when he insisted that she speak frankly, she took a deep breath and told him how she really felt about a couple of the dance routines. He listened very attentively and nodded his head now and again while she was talking, and then he said that those were all very valid and interesting points and he would be sure to tell the rest of the band what she had suggested and see if something couldn't be done about it.

Finally, Stevie stood up.

"Are my eyes red?" he asked

"No, they're *blue!*" Ally exclaimed.

"I mean, from crying."

"Oh, no, no. Sorry. No. Or maybe a tiny bit. But you wouldn't notice unless you looked closely."

"Okay. So have you met the others?"

"Me? No!"

"Where's your friend? The one you came with?"

"Pauline? She's looking for Charlie."

"She won't find him. He's gone."

"Gone?"

"He will have by now. Gone with Caslile. That's what it was all about."

Ally's mouth dropped open.

"Charlie and Caslile!"

"I'm afraid so. Come on. Let's find your friend and I'll introduce you to Nitz and Bobby."

He drank the water, stood up, put the glass in the sink.

"Are you coming then, Ally?"

"Sure, yes, sure. It's just . . ."

"What?"

"I feel a bit nervous."

"Would it help if I took your arm?"

Would it help?

"I'll just go and get Pauline," Ally said, trying to sound calm, but feeling as if there had just been an earthquake.

Ally found Pauline in the bathroom.

"I can't find Charlie anywhere," she said. "I'm dead disappointed."

Ally decided not to tell her about Caslile just then. It would only really upset her and spoil what was left of their time.

"Never mind, I've met someone who says he'll introduce us to Nitz and Bobby R."

"Oh, yeah, who's that?" Pauline said. "Not that bloke in the leather jacket again?"

"Come and meet him, and then you'll see."

"Who is it?"

"Oh, someone, Pauly. Just say it's a surprise."

When one o'clock came, Ally and Pauline said they would have to go.

"My dad'll be worried if we're not back," Ally explained to everyone, "he'll wonder where we are. It's a drag, I know . . ." But all the same, it was good to have someone to worry about you, in some ways.

Stevie saw them to the lift. Everyone shouted to them as they went.

"Goodnight gatecrashers!" Danny Taylor called. He still had his dark glasses on and was acting dead drunk. Lord knows how many beers he'd had.

Stevie joked with the security men about Ally and Pauline getting by.

"Good job they didn't have a gun with them, Rollo," he said.

"Oh, we wouldn't shoot you, Stevie," Pauline said, "not ever."

"Thanks," he said. "I appreciate that. But I wasn't being serious."

"Oh," Pauline said.

She seemed a bit in awe of him. Ally couldn't think why.

The lift doors opened and Ally and Pauline got inside.

"Bye," Stevie said. "Take care."

And wonder of wonders, he kissed them both. Only on the cheek, but it was a kiss all the same.

Yet he didn't say "I must see you again," Ally noticed. He didn't say "I think I've fallen in love." He didn't ask for her phone number and her address. He didn't say all the things he would have said if it had been a story in a magazine. He had his life, she had hers. She felt a pang of loss as the lift descended. It was over now and gone.

"I'll never see him again," Ally said, and tears brimmed in her eyes.

"At least you saw him," Pauline told her. "I never saw Charlie at all."

"He kissed me," Ally said. "Actually kissed me."

"Me too," Pauline said, with a far away look. "Even though I'm more of a Charlie fan. Stevie Manns kissed us."

"I bet he never kissed Marlene Forrester and Tracey Norris," Ally said.

"No fear," Pauline said. "Who'd want to risk it?"

They had forgotten to push the button for the fifteenth floor and so the lift went all the way down to the foyer.

"Let's go and see if my mum and dad are still dancing," Ally said.

"All right," Pauline agreed,

They got out of the lift and went to the dining room. The Hotel Hot Four were still playing – if you could call it playing. Three couples were left on the dance floor and Ally's mum and dad were among them. They had their arms around each other and their eyes were closed, they could almost have been asleep.

"Your mum and dad," said Pauline, "look like they're in love."

"I know," said Ally. "So embarrassing, isn't it? It's enough to make you cringe."

The band was playing a familiar and yet unfamiliar tune. It took a moment before Ally could recognise it. Then she did. Not even the Hotel Hot Four could completely mangle a song as beautiful as that. It was a Five Nine song, the one that Stevie Manns sang. She could hear his voice in her head as he sang.

"Tears cry no more,
No more can I say

I loved you so much
But you went away

Now I'm alone
Alone at your door
Answer my prayer
Tears cry no more."

What did it mean, Ally wondered, *what did it* really
mean? It seemed to mean something different every time
she heard it. Was it a sad song or was it a hopeful one?
Was it a song about loss or was it a song about over-
coming loss and learning to live again, and of making
the best of what was possible and accepting that some
things could never be?

"I think I'll go to bed," Ally said.

"Me too," said Pauline. "It's been a long day."

"The longest ever," Ally said.

"And the best."

"And the worst."

"How do you mean? Not the worst! You met Stevie"

"Yeah, I suppose I did. But—"

"It must have been the happiest day then, surely,
Ally!"

"Yeah," said Ally, "I suppose it was. And yet . . ."

They didn't make it to Stratford-on-Avon the next day
to see Anne Hathaway's cottage. They all slept in too late
and there wasn't the time to go. They made it to the

chocolate factory at Bournville though, as that was closer and more on the way home. They saw all the chocolate being made and got a taste as well.

"Everyone likes chocolate," Ally's dad announced, as they went round. "Did you ever meet anyone who didn't like chocolate? I know plenty of people who *say* they don't like chocolate, but I've never believed them. People say they don't like it, sure, but what they really mean is they're on a diet or something, and not letting themselves have any. I've never met anyone who didn't *really* like chocolate. You can't not like chocolate, can you?"

"That's how the Five Nine are, Dad," Ally said.

He looked perplexed.

"What?" he asked

"Like chocolate," Ally said.

But he didn't really understand.

15

THE END

It was breaktime and the weather was fine, so everybody had gone outside. Some boys were kicking a ball around. Others weren't interested, or couldn't be bothered, and sat and watched, or did something else. Over underneath the horse chestnut tree, Marlene Forrester was holding court.

"And we were introduced to Bobby R," she was saying, "and to Nitz Grey – Nitzy, as we call him –, and—"

"Yeah, so were we," Ally interjected, "we met them too."

Marlene Forrester looked round from her playground bragging to find Ally at her side. Marlene and Tracey Norris had managed to get a huddle of Fine Nine fans around them, all hanging on their every word.

"*You?*" she said scornfully. "*You*, Ally Morgan! Don't make me laugh."

"Yeah, we got invited to the party as well," Pauline told everyone. "And we were there long after *you'd* gone," she said pointedly to Marlene.

"Yeah, you were only there about fifteen minutes,

weren't you?" Ally added. "They were glad to see the back of you. Once you'd gone, they could get the fun started."

"You told us you were there for *hours*, Marlene Forrester!" one of the audience protested. "You fibber!"

And the crowd of playground admirers began to drift away.

"You sure you're not making it all up, Marlene?" Joan Simmons said. "You sure you didn't have a knock on the head?"

"I was *there!* You ask Tracey. It's Ally Morgan who's making it up."

"*We* met Stevie Manns," Pauline said. "And got a kiss on the cheek."

"Liar! You did *not! Show* us it!"

"There!" Pauline said, pointing to her right cheek.

"There's nothing there to see!"

"I didn't say there was."

"What proof have you got then?"

"How about this then?" Ally said. She took out a piece of paper from her coat. It was headed *Azure Hotel Group*. Stevie had torn it off a notepad and had scribbled on it for her.

To Ally Morgan, it read. *Tears cry no more. And only you know why. All my love and all my thanks forever. Your biggest fan, Stevie Manns.*

People stared at it in wonder, like it was the holy grail.

Marlene Forrester peered at it critically. She went to take it, but Ally wouldn't let it go.

"It's a forgery," Marlene said. "She wrote that herself."

"Just a minute," Joan Simmons said, "I've got the newsletter here."

She took out the official Five Nine fan club monthly newsletter from her folder. The newsletter was always signed by Bobby R, Nitz, Charlie and Stevie. She compared the Stevie signature on the hotel notepaper with the facsimile on the newsletter.

"Sorry, Marlene," she said. "Looks genuine to me."

"Huh!" Marlene said. "Well, me and Tracey had a better time there!"

"Doesn't sound like it," Joan said.

"How would *you* know anyway?!" said Marlene. "And besides, I'm going off the Five Nine anyway. They're just getting to be old stuff now."

"The Five Nine are forever," Ally said. "Forever and for always."

"Well, I'm not renewing *my* fan club membership, I can tell you that," Marlene pouted.

"I bet they'll be relieved about that," Pauline commented, drily.

"Boyz For Real are better anyway," Marlene said.

"Boyz For Real?" Joan Simmons said, incredulously. "Boyz For Real are a bunch of pimples! They're kids' stuff. That's for little girlies."

"Fat lot *you* know then, don't you?" Marlene said. "Come on, Tracey," she said, and they both stomped off across the playground in search of other friends – who at that moment were in rather short supply.

Pauline had to take a book back to the school library then and so Ally was left on her own. She sat on the wall and looked out from the playground to the world beyond.

One day I'll be out there, she thought. *What'll I do? What'll be?*

A hairdresser like her sister? She didn't think so. And Cheryl was getting married soon too. She and Michael had announced their engagement shortly after Ally and her parents had returned from Birmingham.

Cheryl, getting married, and she wasn't even twenty. *What'll I do? What'll I be?*

I'll try to be someone, she thought, *I'll try to do something*. But who she would be and what she would become, it was all so hazy and vague.

Maybe she'd be a career woman. Then maybe after a while she'd marry someone and have children. Or maybe not have children. Or maybe she wouldn't marry. Maybe they'd just live together and she'd refer to him as *my partner*. Maybe it would last forever, in a mum and dad kind of way. Maybe it would all go wrong and they'd split up. You had to think about it. Maybe she'd break his heart. Maybe he'd break hers. Yes, maybe her heart would be broken and she would have to start again. The way Stevie had to start again.

The way we all have to start again.

You never knew. Nothing was certain. It was like in the songs. Bitter-sweet. Sweet and sour. Sad and happy. All mixed up together.

Oh Stevie, oh Stevie, oh Stevie, I love you so much. Why couldn't you have loved me too? Why doesn't it work out like that? Why doesn't it, Stevie? Do you know?

While she was there thinking, Phil Roach came along and sat on the wall next to her. After a minute he spoke.

"Ally . . ."

"Phil."

He swallowed hard.

"Ally . . ."

"What?"

"Would you come out with me one night? To the cinema or something? Or for a coffee?"

She didn't reply at first. She just sat and stared at him. He had a nice face really. Quite nice-looking. A bit like Stevie Manns in some respects, with strong cheekbones and an almost – but not quite – dimpled chin. He smiled. And it was a nice smile, even if he didn't have blue eyes. His eyes were hazel, which was a nice colour too, in its way. He wasn't Stevie, of course. Never would be, never could be. But the good thing about him was that he didn't pretend to be either. He was himself. Just as Ally was herself. And that was all you could be, wasn't it? Yourself. That was the best you could do.

"How about it then, Ally? Maybe Friday? The cinema?"

"All right," she said. "I'll come with you."

"Great," he said. "I'll pick you up, then, shall I? At your house? Seven o'clock?"

"Fine," she said.

"Great! I'll see you then."

"And Phil . . ."

"Yeah?"

"Thanks for asking me."

"Thanks for saying you'd come, Ally."

Phil got down from the wall and walked away. Ally watched him go. What if he felt about her the way that she had felt – still felt – about Stevie? What if *he* was in love with *her*?

As he went, he began to whistle. Ally recognised the tune. It was a Five Nine number. She smiled and returned to her class.

Two months later the Five Nine split up. Bobby R went on to have a few hit records on his own and to write songs for other artists. Stevie went into production and Nitz joined another band.

Caslile and Charlie got married and they had a baby girl. They called her Mountain Dew. It was an unusual choice of name, but some people feel that they have to be different, and pop stars and models are often among them, and they hang on to being different the way that skydivers hang on to parachutes.

A year has passed. Phil and Ally are still seeing each other, and Boyz For Real are number one right now. Their lead singer is called Flame. He only has the one name, not two names, like the rest of us. You wouldn't believe how many people are in love with him though, and he is very good-looking.

But Ally doesn't reckon much on Boyz For Real. And neither does Pauline. they look at the younger girls in the school going mad over them and can't really see what the fuss is about.

"It's only a crush," Ally said once. "That's all it is. Just schoolgirl infatuation. They don't know what real love means."

Pauline was too good a friend to let her get away with that.

"Not the way we know, eh, Ally?" she said with a smile. "You and Stevie? Me and Charlie? It's all right for us experts."

Ally paused before smiling back. "Yeah," she said. "Maybe you're right. Who does know, Pauline? Who does know what real love is? Who really knows for sure?"

But the bell rang then for the end of break. And she never did get an answer.

crush (krush): v.t.   to break or bruise
                                     to squeeze together
                                     to subdue
                                     to ruin

                 n.   a violent squeezing
                                     a close crowd of persons
                                     or things
                                     a drink made from fruit juice
                                     an infatuation

           Alex Shearer (with thanks to
                 the dictionary)